FOR THE SAKE OF WARWICK MOUNTAIN

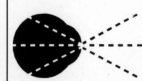

This Large Print Book carries the
Seal of Approval of N.A.V.H.

FOR THE SAKE OF WARWICK MOUNTAIN

CHARLOTTE DOUGLAS

THORNDIKE PRESS

A part of Gale, Cengage Learning

GALE
CENGAGE Learning·

Farmington Hills, Mich • San Francisco • New York • Waterville, Maine
Meriden, Conn • Mason, Ohio • Chicago

GALE
CENGAGE Learning®

Copyright © 2012 by Charlotte H. Douglas.
Originally published as DR. WONDERFUL
Copyright © 2003 by Charlotte H. Douglas
Thorndike Press, a part of Gale, Cengage Learning.

ALL RIGHTS RESERVED
This is a work of fiction. Names, characters, places, and incidents are either the product of the author's imagination or are used fictitiously, and any resemblance to actual persons, living or dead, business establishments, events or locales is entirely coincidental.
Thorndike Press® Large Print Cleans Reads.
The text of this Large Print edition is unabridged.
Other aspects of the book may vary from the original edition.
Set in 16 pt. Plantin.

LIBRARY OF CONGRESS CATALOGING-IN-PUBLICATION DATA

Douglas, Charlotte.
  [Dr. Wonderful]
  For the sake of Warwick Mountain / by Charlotte Douglas. -- Large Print edition.
    pages cm. -- (Thorndike Press Large Print Clean Reads)
    ISBN 978-1-4104-6817-8 (hardcover) -- ISBN 1-4104-6817-8 (hardcover)
    1. Blue Ridge Mountains--Fiction. 2. Public health--Fiction. 3. Rural health clinics--Fiction. 4. Large type books. I. Title.
  PS3604.O9254F67 2014
  813'.6--dc23   2013050600

Published in 2014 by arrangement with Harlequin Books S.A.

Printed in Mexico
1 2 3 4 5 6 7 18 17 16 15 14

FOR THE SAKE OF
WARWICK MOUNTAIN

CHAPTER ONE

The house was finally ready for company.

With a sigh of weary satisfaction, Rebecca Warwick sank into the rocking chair beside the crackling fire in the mammoth stone fireplace. Shoving a strand of honey-colored hair off her forehead, she sipped a well-earned cup of tea. In spite of the drizzling rain pattering on the roof, the low-ceilinged room of the centuries-old log mountain house was snug and warm. It was also immaculately clean for the very important guest who would be arriving tomorrow for a month's stay.

Becca smiled in anticipation of the elderly doctor's visit. Dwight Peyseur had lived in her house for a month last summer while providing much-needed free medical care to their isolated community deep in the North Carolina mountains. During that time, she and Emily, her four-and-a-half-year-old daughter, had come to think of him

7

not only as a compassionate physician but also a kindly grandfather, a member of the family. They were looking forward to his arrival tomorrow morning.

In spite of her longing for a bath to wash away the dust and grime from her cleaning spree, Becca couldn't force herself to leave the comfort of her chair. She seldom took the opportunity to sit a spell and relax, as her granny used to say. But school was out for summer vacation, Emily was down for her nap, and leftovers in the fridge relieved Becca of the need to begin preparing supper. With a luxurious stretch, she set her cup aside, settled deeper into the chair, and promptly nodded off to sleep.

A relentless banging at the front door jerked her from her slumber.

Anxious to stop the racket before it awakened Emily, Becca leaped from the chair and hurried to the entry. With her heart pounding from her rude awakening and her mind wondering what dire emergency had precipitated such an uproar, she yanked open the heavy door.

The man before her drove all thoughts from her head, but was no deterrent to her thundering heart.

A tall, broad-shouldered stranger gazed across the front yard toward a Land Rover parked by the gate. Even though she couldn't see his face, Becca recognized immediately that the man was an outsider, definitely not one of her many neighbors and kin who lived in the surrounding hills and hollows of Warwick Mountain.

He didn't wear worn jeans or overalls, faded chambray shirts or scuffed work boots that were the common uniform of those who farmed the steep, rocky terrain. In fact, the man looked as if he'd never had a close encounter with dirt, much less hard labor, in his entire life. His expensive khaki slacks were unwrinkled, his muted madras shirt the finest cotton, and his Italian loafers shone as if they'd just been polished. His thick brown hair had obviously been professionally styled, and the gold watch on his wrist would probably feed a mountain family of six for a full year.

Remembering her manners, Becca asked, "May I help you?"

She assumed the man was lost, having taken by mistake the long, winding road that dead-ended in the village, and then followed the gravel road to her house.

He turned at the sound of her voice, and when he faced her, she felt the air leave her lungs as surely as if someone had driven a fist into her stomach. His sun-streaked, mahogany-colored hair, slightly dampened by the rain, fell across a broad forehead above a pair of magnificent eyes as deep and brown as the river that ran through the back forty acres. With his golden tan, lean muscular build and a slow, easy smile that made her insides quiver, he looked every inch a quintessential California surfer, aged to a marvelous thirtyish maturity.

"I'm looking for Rebecca Warwick." His voice was deep and warm and she took a moment to register his words.

"Why?" she asked in surprise, once she'd recovered breath enough to speak.

"I'm supposed to stay in her home. I understand she's the local schoolteacher."

Becca shook away the confusion the handsome man's arrival and unexpected query had caused. "I'm Rebecca Warwick." She noted that the pupils in his remarkable eyes dilated with apparent shock at her admission. "But there must be some mistake —"

"*You're* Rebecca Warwick? The teacher?" Disbelief tinged his voice and showed clearly in his expression.

She shrugged, smiled and tried to make light of his skepticism. "Last time I checked. You can see my driver's license if you want proof."

He shook his head, his eyes clouded with

confusion. "Didn't Dr. Peyseur call you?"

"No one's called. The phones have been out since last night's storm."

"Don't you have a cell phone?" His expression turned even more incredulous.

Becca's smile widened at his disbelief. "The surrounding mountains block the signals. Cell phones aren't much use here." Her smile disappeared. "Why was Dr. Peyseur supposed to call me?"

The stranger shook his head again in obvious frustration. "I'm sorry. Dwight promised he'd let you know he can't make his annual trip."

Disappointment cascaded through her, not only for her own loss at his canceled visit but for the continued suffering of those his medical attention would have helped. "Why can't he come? Is he all right?"

The man's eyes glowed with warm sympathy. "As all right as he can be with a broken wrist."

"Oh, no. That's awful. How —" Then, suddenly recalling what her visitor had mentioned earlier, she raised an eyebrow. "You said *you're* supposed to stay with me?"

"Sorry. I didn't mean to barge in unannounced. I was expecting Dwight to pave the way." With an ingratiating look that warmed her to her toes, he offered his hand.

"I'm Matthew Tyler, Dr. Peyseur's partner. I'll be filling in for him, since he can't perform surgery with his wrist broken."

When Matthew Tyler grasped her fingers, they tingled with a strange warmth, as if a jolt of electricity had arced between her and the attractive stranger, and she found herself momentarily tongue-tied. Regarding him from beneath lowered eyelids, she wished for her grandmother's gift of second sight. Granny Warwick would have known in an instant exactly what this handsome stranger's motives were, why he'd come to Warwick Mountain and what he'd accomplish, for good or ill, while he was here.

Becca, however, had inherited only a fraction of her grandmother's gift. While she couldn't predict the future as Granny had, she could read people fairly well upon first meeting them. For an instant, she perused Matthew Tyler as if he were a fascinating book.

Knows what he wants and gets it. Extroverted. Believes in himself and his abilities. Boundless ambition. High energy. Temper shows when he's pushed to his limits. Goodhearted —

"May I have it back now?"

He gently tugged his fingers from hers, and she flushed with embarrassment at being so absorbed in her reading, she had forgotten she held on to his hand. But at the end, right before she'd broken contact, she'd sensed something else, something deeply hidden, a sense of intense dissatisfaction that Matthew Tyler tried to deny existed. She'd lost the vibes, however, before she could identify the source of his discontent, and her unfulfilled curiosity hummed with interest — until she tamped it down.

She didn't intend to find *any* man interesting. An interesting man would add complications to her life she neither needed nor desired.

Remembering her Southern hospitality, however, she stepped back and opened the door wider. "You'd better come in out of the rain."

When she moved aside for him to enter, she caught a glimpse of herself in the mirror in the entry hall. Her hair, caught back from her face by a bandanna kerchief, was a mass of tangled curls, dust smudged her cheek, and the clothes she had chosen for her housecleaning were faded and shabby. Not exactly the attire she'd have selected for meeting the best-looking man she'd ever seen.

Not that his looks mattered. She'd been vaccinated for life against the wiles of handsome, wealthy men by the heartbreak Grady had put her through.

Then why is your heart pounding as if you just climbed Lovers' Peak at a run? her conscience demanded.

Becca chalked up her accelerated pulse to unfulfilled curiosity and concern for Dr. Peyseur. No way was she ever letting a charmer affect her life again. Once burned, twice shy, and she'd been torched for life.

"Dr. Peyseur wasn't due until tomorrow," she explained. "I wasn't expecting —"

"He was supposed to alert you that I'd arrive early, but with the phones out . . ." He shrugged his broad shoulders, and concern etched the handsome lines of his face. "If you're not prepared, I'll stay at a motel. Is there one in town?"

Becca shook her head. "You passed through town to reach here."

His eyes widened again with shock. "You call that a town?"

"A village. There's just the Shop-N-Go convenience market and gas station and the Baptist church. And the old feed store that's closed now. The nearest motel or bed-and-breakfast is over forty miles away."

He raised an eyebrow in misgiving. "Back down that sorry excuse for a road that had me hanging off the sides of mountains to get here?"

She nodded and suppressed a smile. The narrow, winding mountain roads were especially daunting to those who weren't used to them. "But a motel won't be necessary. Your room is ready."

Even as she said the words, she experienced a shiver of reluctance. In Warwick Mountain, everyone knew everybody else's business. Having an elderly and respected doctor staying with her and Emily was one thing, but to share her house with the handsome man beside her for a month — unchaperoned — would have every tongue for miles wagging in disapproval.

Especially Aunt Delilah Bennett's.

Aunt Delilah had yet to forgive the previous scandal Becca had caused over five years earlier, one that had rocked the small community to its core. The hardworking, impoverished people of Warwick Mountain were kind and generous, but they adhered unswervingly to a strict moral code. Only with Granny Warwick as her staunch champion had Becca managed to survive their disapproval. Not only survive, but eventually to earn the respect and admiration of neighbors who had initially shunned her. The last thing she needed was more notoriety. For her dreams to reach fruition, she

15

had to keep her reputation intact.

The prospect of once again being the center of such intense scrutiny and public censure because a handsome stranger was residing under her roof might have been enough for Becca to send the attractive Dr. Matthew Tyler packing, down the treacherous road he'd found so formidable. She wanted him off the mountain, back to wherever he'd come from.

Until she remembered little Lizzie McClain, the main focus of Dr. Peyseur's intended visit.

Against Lizzie's problems, Becca's dilemma seemed insignificant. She could endure again the nasty gossip, raised eyebrows and her pious neighbors' chilly disapproval if having Dr. Tyler in her home meant curing Lizzie of her horrible affliction.

Then she thought of Emily.

At age four-going-on-five, her daughter was old enough to realize if the neighbors turned their backs on her mother. Even for Lizzie McClain's and Jimmy Dickens's sake, Becca couldn't put Emily through the trauma of ostracism. At Emily's tender stage of development, the emotional impact of seeing her mother cast out could scar her for life.

Becca squared her shoulders. Fate had thrown her a curve in the form of Dr. Matthew Tyler, but, for Lizzie's sake, Becca would find a way to deal with the problem. Too late to make other arrangements today, though. The man could stay this one night. He was nothing to her, after all, but Dr. Peyseur's replacement, a healer who had come to help the community. She would keep her distance, polite and appreciative but aloof, and locate another place for the doctor to board tomorrow.

Maybe with Aunt Delilah. Or Cousin Bessie. Or even Preacher Evans and his wife. In the meantime, if tongues wagged and eyebrows lifted, they were their owners' problems, not hers.

She assumed her most hospitable expression. "It won't take a minute to make fresh coffee. Would you like some?"

The radiance of his Hollywood-perfect smile lit the gloomy room. "Thanks. It'll chase away the chill from the rain. Is it always this cold here in June?"

"Not always. Sometimes it's scorching. Weather changes all the time." What was wrong with her? She was babbling like an idiot. "Make yourself comfortable by the fire. I'll be right back."

She hurried to the kitchen, wet a paper

17

towel, scrubbed the dust from her cheeks, stripped off her kerchief and ran her fingers through her hair in an unsuccessful attempt to tame its chaos. Not that she cared how she looked to her visitor. She simply had her own standards to maintain.

The entire time she was preparing coffee, however, she couldn't escape the niggling feeling that she had seen Matthew Tyler somewhere before. But that was impossible. His and Dr. Peyseur's practice was in Beverly Hills, California, a place she'd never visited.

Taking a full mug, she returned to the living room where her guest had settled in the overstuffed chair beside the hearth. She handed him his coffee. "Here you are, Dr. Tyler."

"Call me Matt."

His friendly smile lifted the corners of his mouth and lit his eyes, brown as molten caramel. She was glad her grandmother's rocker was there to catch her when her knees weakened. She needed to turn the conversation quickly to a safe topic to quell her reaction to the man's charisma, which was probably part of his usual bedside manner. Enough nonsense, she told herself — she wasn't some hormone-driven teenager, but a mature woman in her late twenties.

Time she acted like one. "Tell me about Dr. Peyseur. How did he break his wrist?"

She focused on the kindly doctor's injury to keep her head from whirling. She'd worn herself out cleaning house, that was all. Breathed too many cleaning-fluid vapors. The chemicals had to be influencing her. She'd learned too much the hard way to allow any man to affect her as Matthew Tyler seemed to.

Apparently unaware of her inner turmoil, Matt sipped his coffee. "Dwight tripped on a garden hose while fetching his morning paper. Managed to break his fall with his right hand, but his wrist took the brunt. He'll be in a cast for six weeks. Maybe longer."

"Bones don't heal fast at his age." Worry for her old friend filled her. "He lives alone. How will he manage?"

Matt's eyes twinkled. "He doesn't live alone any longer. I saw to that."

"How?" She hoped he hadn't confined the old doctor to a nursing home. Dwight Peyseur loved his independence too much to adjust to such a routine.

"Hired him a housekeeper," Matt said.

Becca thought back to what the older doctor had shared with her about his life. After his wife had died ten years ago, he had continued to live in their Beverly Hills home. He ate his meals out, and he had a cleaning service that came once a week. "I thought he already had someone who takes care of the house."

The twinkle danced a little faster in Matt's striking eyes. "Mrs. Sanderingham is different."

In spite of her best efforts, Becca couldn't keep the blush from flaring in her cheeks. "You're not suggesting —"

"Not suggesting a thing. But I admit to playing matchmaker." Oozing self-confidence and satisfaction, he leaned back in his chair and stretched his long legs in front of him. "Dwight's been alone too long since Madeline died. Mrs. Sanderingham is not only a registered nurse, an excellent cook and a superb housekeeper, she's exactly the kind of witty, intelligent woman Dwight needs in his life."

"*Mrs.* Sanderingham?"

Annoyance stirred inside her. Matt Tyler had a nerve to force unwanted attention from a strange woman onto his partner. Becca knew all too well the irritation well-meaning meddlers could wreak on a person's life. When it came to matchmakers, Aunt Delilah considered herself world class. Becca was constantly fending off attention from so-called eligible men her aunt aimed her way.

"From what Dr. Peyseur told me," she said with more vexation in her tone than she'd intended, "he enjoys his solitude. That's why he likes being here so much. In fact, he also said that no woman could ever take Madeline's place."

Matt nodded agreeably. "Quite right. And I'm sure Dwight could never replace Mr. Sanderingham. That doesn't mean the two can't enjoy each other's company."

"Do you live alone?" Becca regretted the question the moment it left her lips. Her query was not only rude, but unnecessary. Matt Tyler's living arrangements were no concern of hers.

Except for the next month, she corrected herself. Unless she could make other arrangements, he'd be sleeping in Granny Warwick's black walnut poster bed, one floor directly beneath her own.

"I'm not married, if that's what you're asking," Matt replied easily, amused by her curiosity.

He took another sip of coffee, decided it tasted even better than the Starbucks he favored, and finished the cup. He hoped he'd managed to hide his surprise earlier when the enchanting woman across from him had announced that *she* was Rebecca Warwick.

Dwight had explained that Miss Warwick was the schoolteacher in this godforsaken backwoods, and Matt had expected an elderly crone with a neck like a chicken, a figure like a stick and a voice like gravel.

Man, had he had it all wrong.

Rebecca Warwick didn't come anywhere close to his misconception. In fact, she was very appealing, in spite of the fact that her emerald-green eyes were a shade too far apart, her mouth a bit too wide and her nose turned up a tad too much at the tip. He assessed her with a plastic surgeon's eye. The proportions of her slim figure were classic, and the prominent cheekbones of her heart-shaped face would turn any Hollywood starlet green with envy. The satiny smoothness of her peaches-and-cream complexion defied improvement by even the most skilled movie-makeup artist. Even though her thick mane of golden-brown hair framing her face in a tangle of curls would make Matt's stylist run for his scissors, her tousled look held an undeniable charm.

But only from a strictly professional viewpoint. After all, he'd seen enough female pulchritude in his practice to remain relatively unimpressed by gorgeous women. And she wasn't the most beautiful woman he'd ever seen.

Then why couldn't he take his eyes off her?

"More coffee?" she asked, and he amended her list of attributes to include a voice as silky smooth as the finest bourbon with just a hint of a Southern drawl.

"Thanks." He cooled his jets, handed her his cup, then watched her retreat into the kitchen for a refill.

Shaking himself out of his dazed surprise at Miss Warwick's being far from the white-haired, homely spinster he'd envisioned, he contemplated the situation he found himself in so unexpectedly. In spite of his appealing hostess, he really didn't want to be here, not in the cold, gloomy drizzle of the Smoky Mountains.

Smoky?

Gray and dreary were more appropriate, and the damp penetrated to his bones. Right now he'd intended to be sunning himself on the teakwood deck of a chartered yacht anchored off the coast of Fiji. But how was he supposed to say no to his best friend and mentor? Dwight was such a good guy, how could Matt turn him down, even when it meant giving up the vacation he'd been looking forward to for months? A vacation he desperately needed to drive away the deep dissatisfaction that had haunted him lately.

A discontent he was certain that time off in the right locale with the proper amenities and pleasing company could cure. He was tired and could use a rest. Although he didn't begrudge the people of Warwick Mountain the medical care they seriously needed, he felt like a bucket that had been drained dry with nothing left to give. His problem had to be fatigue. His life, after all, was as perfect as a life could be. He had gained international acclaim as a plastic surgeon, had more money than he could spend in his lifetime, an enviable Malibu beach house and a full social calendar. What more could a man want?

A vacation.

Which he wasn't going to have, thanks to Dwight. Guilt stabbed at him when he considered his friend's broken bone. It wasn't as if Dwight had fractured his wrist on purpose to sabotage Matt's cruise.

He shook off his gloomy thoughts. If he could finish Dwight's work in Warwick Mountain quickly, regardless of the slow mountain pace Dwight had warned him about, Matt might still find time for that vacation.

"Who are you?" A high, shrill voice sounded beside him, jolting him from his thoughts.

Standing by the arm of his chair was a miniature version of Rebecca Warwick. The little girl with round green eyes alight with curiosity — and more than a hint of suspicion — and a riot of honey-brown curls had to be related to the schoolteacher. A younger sister?

"I'm Matt. Who are you?"

"Emily."

He considered the tyke with interest. No more than about five years old, from the flush on her face, her tousled hair and feet clad only in socks, she apparently had just awakened from a nap.

"Do you live here?" When Dwight had told him Rebecca Warwick was single, Matt had assumed the teacher lived alone.

"Uh-huh." Emily climbed into the rocker beside the fire and sat with her feet sticking just over the edge of the seat.

When he'd first arrived at the Warwick house, Matt had noted that wings had been added to the original log building and now wondered how many other residents filled its rooms. "Who else lives here?"

"Just Mommy and me."

"Mommy?"

Emily nodded. "She's a teacher. But not now. It's summer."

"So just the two of you live in this big house?" His interest was piqued. Where was Emily's father?

"Granny went to heaven," Emily announced solemnly.

"I'm sorry."

The little girl shook her head. "Mommy says don't be sad. Granny's in a pretty place. Her heart doesn't hurt now."

Emily was a charmer with a vivacious personality. Intelligence sparkled in her green eyes. Matt couldn't resist another question. "Where's your daddy?"

Emily shifted her weight to make her chair rock. "Don't have a daddy."

Glancing past Emily toward the kitchen door, Matt spotted Rebecca standing there, her face a blank mask, and wondered if she'd overheard his questions.

When her gaze met his, she hurried into the room. "Here's your coffee. I see you've met Emily."

His hostess gave no indication that his third degree of her daughter had rattled her, except for the slight hint of breathlessness in her voice.

"Dwight didn't mention Emily," Matt said. "Although, come to think of it, that must be why he sent two presents with me. Must be one for each of you." He set his cup aside. "They're in my luggage. I'll get them."

Rebecca's face flushed, and she shifted her feet with obvious uneasiness. "Dr. Tyler —"

"It's Matt, remember?"

"Before you unpack your car, we need to talk."

Maybe his inquiries to Emily had offended Rebecca more than he'd realized. He settled back in his chair. "I'm listening."

Before Rebecca could utter another word, the front door flew open, and a small, wiry woman burst into the room and headed for Rebecca.

Remembering the manners his mother had drilled into him as a child, Matt pushed to his feet, but the woman didn't seem to notice him.

"Has Dr. Peyseur already arrived?" the newcomer asked. "I saw the car out front, and I brought him a chocolate pound cake."

"Dwight can't come," Rebecca announced. "He broke his wrist. This is Dr. Tyler, his partner. He's taking Dr. Peyseur's place."

The gray-haired woman faced Matt, and her eyes lit with recognition. Her mouth fell open and the cake bobbled in her hands. She saved it from crashing to the floor with a maneuver that would have made an NFL wide receiver proud. Shifting the captured plate to one hand, she grabbed Rebecca's elbow with the other and dragged the young woman with her toward the kitchen. Before Matt could say anything, the door slammed behind them.

"That's Aunt Delilah," Emily announced matter-of-factly, as if her relative always descended on the house with the speed and fury of a whirlwind.

Matt sank back into his chair, curious over Delilah's obvious negative reaction to him. Maybe she was one of the bevy of older women who found Dwight so attractive and was disappointed that he'd been replaced.

"You've got to get that man out of here!" In spite of the closed door, Delilah's hysterical tone carried clearly into the living room.

"Shh, he'll hear you," Matt heard Rebecca's hushed and slightly frantic reply.

"He can't stay in this house." Her niece's warning had failed to lower Delilah's volume. "Don't you know who he is?"

"He's Matthew Tyler, Dwight's partner," Rebecca answered in a reasonable tone.

28

"Oh, no, he's much worse than that!"

Emily, also tuned in to the conversation in the kitchen, studied Matt with renewed interest.

"What are you talking about?" Rebecca asked.

"He's Dr. Wonderful," Delilah said in a tone that seemed to equate the nickname with evil incarnate. "You've got to get him out of this house. Now."

CHAPTER TWO

Becca rescued the cake plate from Aunt Delilah's hands when it wobbled precariously a second time and placed it safely on the counter.

"Dr. Wonderful?" She cast a worried look at the door between her and the room where Matt Tyler sat with Emily. "What are you talking about?"

Before her great-aunt could answer, Becca edged her toward the far end of the kitchen in hopes her guest wouldn't overhear their conversation.

Aunt Delilah settled onto the bench in the bay window of the breakfast nook, fanned her heated face with one hand and clasped her heart with the other. "I can't believe you've never heard of him."

Becca slid onto the bench across from her. Although Granny's younger sister looked enough like her grandmother to be her twin — small, wiry frame, luxuriant gray hair that refused to remain in a sedate bun and wily gray eyes that sparked with wisdom — their personalities were as different as night from day. Where Granny had been calm and unflappable, Delilah's moods were as mercurial as the mountain weather, sunny and bright one moment, gloomy and stormy the next. The sisters held in common, however, their deep abiding love of family and the land from which generations of Warwicks had sprung. What affected one touched all, and Aunt Delilah always rose to a perceived threat to protect her clan like a mama bear with cubs.

She leaned across the table, her gray eyes snapping like thunderclouds laced with heat lightning. "That man was on the cover of *People* magazine just last month."

That's where she'd seen him, Becca recalled. On the magazine cover in the beauty shop that Cousin Bessie ran out of the front room of her house. Becca pictured the gleaming smile, the handsome face — then forced the image from her mind to concentrate on what her aunt was saying.

"That man has more money than God. The article said he's the doctor to the stars. Showed pictures of him with bunches of young celebrities, most of them with bosoms out to here —" Delilah held her hands a foot from her own flat chest "— and some in bikinis that should have had them arrested for indecent exposure. He's dated most of Hollywood's prettiest women."

Becca blinked in surprise. "The magazine actually said that?"

"Of course not." Her aunt gave an impatient shake of her head that loosed another gray curl from her bun. "His lawyers would be on them like a duck on a june bug if they had, but I could read between the lines. The man's a lothario. That's why he can't stay in your house. He'll ruin your reputation." She gave a self-righteous sniff. "What little of it you have left after your escapades in Pinehurst all those years ago."

Becca flinched at her aunt's bluntness, but she knew Delilah didn't mean to be unkind. She was merely concerned for the welfare of her great-niece.

"I've already reached the same conclusion," Becca said.

"That he's a lothario?" Delilah's eyes widened in alarm. "He hasn't tried anything —"

"No, he's been the picture of perfect manners." Matt hadn't had to do anything, Becca thought. Just his knock-'em-dead appearance and his compelling charm were enough to catch the attention of any woman who wasn't blind and deaf. Any woman except herself, of course, since she'd sworn off all men since Grady. "But it wouldn't be fitting for him to board here with Emily and me. I don't need to give the community more fuel for gossip."

Delilah sat back on the bench with a sigh. "That's a relief. I'm glad you're being sensible about this. You weren't the last time, you know."

Becca shut out memories of that painful past and focused on today's dilemma. Her aunt had provided the perfect opening for Becca's request. "That's why I want him to stay with you and Uncle Jake."

"What?" Her aunt reacted as if Becca had dropped a load of bricks on her.

Becca smiled. "With your sterling reputation and Uncle Jake to act as watchdog, you're the perfect couple to host Dr. Wonderful while he fills in for Dr. Peyseur."

Varying emotions scurried across Aunt Delilah's milk-and-roses complexion, still lovely in spite of the fine lines seventy-eight years of clean living had etched there. "I'd love to help you, but I can't."

Panic squeezed Becca's chest. "Why not? You have that beautiful spare room —"

"It's not spare anymore. Jake brought his sister, Lydia, up from Blairsville yesterday.

Her sciatica has her bedridden — in our guest room. According to the doctors, it could be weeks before she's on her feet again."

"Then maybe Cousin Bessie —"

"Not a chance. That poor woman's on her feet all day at the beauty parlor. She doesn't have the strength left to wait on company. Besides, you know how jealous Frank is. He wouldn't tolerate the man in his house."

Becca was grasping at straws. "The preacher and his wife have room —"

"They're leaving tomorrow for a pulpit exchange with a church in Bryson City. The Bryson City preacher's coming here with a wife and five children. Won't be room for a guest."

"There has to be someone who can board him." Becca couldn't believe the predicament that faced her.

Her aunt shook her head. "Not many who'd want to, knowing his infamous reputation."

"How can they know if we don't tell them?" Becca asked in frustration.

"Every woman who has her hair done at Bessie's knows. Bessie had two copies of that issue in her shop. And they were both dog-eared and well read, let me tell you."

Becca felt the old rebellion rising inside

her. "Then he'll just have to stay here. I won't deny people medical care for fear of a bunch of gossipy old women."

Delilah's eyes glowed with sympathy. "Your motives are good, honey, but you can't sacrifice yourself. You have Emily to think of."

"That's true. I don't want Emily's feelings hurt."

"I wasn't thinking of Emily's feelings. It's your job I'm worried about. You know how the school board is. They set a higher standard for their teachers than anyone else. How will you support Emily if you lose your job?"

"How will I face Lizzie McClain and Jimmy Dickens if I turn away their best chance for a healthy, happy life?" Irrational anger at the man in the next room surged through her. Why couldn't he have been old, stodgy and ugly as homemade sin, as well as one of the world's most brilliant plastic surgeons?

"Maybe Dr. Peyseur will come next year," her aunt said.

"Do you remember how long a year is to a child? Especially an unhappy child?" Becca buried her face in her hands and accepted the blow fate had dealt her. She had no choice. She couldn't sacrifice her own daughter's welfare for the other children, no matter how needy they were. She had to keep her job to support Emily.

She was all Emily had.

She rose from the bench and squared her shoulders. "Well, that's that, then. I'll tell him he has to leave."

Her aunt stood and hugged her in a fierce embrace. "I'm sorry, honey. I know how much all the children of this community mean to you. But you have yourself and Emily to consider. You've made the right choice. Enjoy the cake. I'll let myself out the back."

As the screen door slammed behind Aunt Delilah, Becca sank onto the bench. If she'd made the right choice, why did it feel so wrong?

Matt suffered a pang of disappointment when the women in the kitchen moved farther from the door and cut off his access to their conversation. Their discussion had just been getting interesting.

With a scowl, he recalled the nickname "Doctor Wonderful," the invention of the feature writer who'd interviewed him for a recent magazine article. The name lacked dignity and made him feel like some kind of comic-book character, but once the publication had hit the stands, the distasteful moniker had stuck. Maybe its unwanted notoriety was part of the dissatisfaction he'd felt so keenly recently.

"Are you Dr. Wonderful?" Emily asked.

Matt shook his head. "I'm Dr. Tyler."

"Did Aunt Delilah tell a lie?" A sharp discernment shone in the tiny girl's big green eyes.

"No. Dr. Wonderful is a nickname someone gave me, but I don't like it, so I don't use it. Do you have a nickname?"

Emily nodded. "Granny used to call me Sweet Pea. I like Emily better."

Sweet Pea suited her. The child was a sweetheart. He'd never paid much attention to children before. Never saw them in his practice, because Dwight treated the youngsters. But this little girl touched his emotions in a way that surprised him.

"So," Matt said with a smile, "you understand what I mean about nicknames."

"I guess." She wrinkled her nose as if deep in thought. "If Dr. Dwight isn't coming, are you going to stay with us?"

Matt cocked his head but couldn't distinguish anything more from the murmur of voices behind the kitchen door. "I guess that's up to your mother and Aunt Delilah."

"I hope you stay," she said with earnestness. "You'll like it. It's nice here."

Matt glanced around the room, its low ceiling supported by hand-hewn beams. It seemed ancient and small, lacking the style of his Malibu home with its fourteen-foot ceilings, expansive glass walls overlooking the Pacific and the sparse elegance of chrome and glass his interior designer had insisted on. Matt's house was the perfect place for a party, but he'd need a crowbar and a shoehorn to fit even a dozen people into this room.

Still, the mountain house had a certain charm. Earthernware jugs held casual bouquets of wild flowers, roses and a fragrant blooming vine that were a drastic counterpoint to the stark ikebana twig and orchid arrangements in his own home.

The rug on the highly polished floor of wide oak planks was hand braided, its colors muted by time and wear. Schoolteachers were underpaid, but made enough to afford more than Rebecca Warwick apparently had. What made her stay in this poverty-stricken pocket of the mountains?

The thought of poverty triggered memories of his boyhood. He'd never known his father, who'd died when Matt was two. The home his mother had kept had been old and well lived in, like this room. Money had been tight then. Tight? It hadn't existed, and Matt had sworn once he grew up, he'd see that his and his mother's lives would be better. His mother hadn't lived long enough for him to make good his promise to her, but he'd worked hard for his success and the expensive trappings that accompanied it.

He leaned back in the worn, overstuffed chair that in spite of, or because of, its age seemed to embrace him, and an unusual sensation hit him, one he couldn't remember experiencing for a long time.

Relaxation.

Something in the atmosphere of the mountain house, maybe a combination of the cheerful crackle of the fire and the soft patter of rain against the windows, had bled the tension from his muscles and the worries from his mind. Almost as effectively as a South Pacific cruise.

Almost, but not quite. He really needed that vacation.

"Yes," he assured Emily, who was staring at him as if waiting for a response, "your house is very nice."

Thinking of his canceled cruise and the South Pacific sun he was missing, he itched again to finish Dwight's work in a hurry so he could squeeze in that much-needed R and R.

The sound of a screen door slamming somewhere in the house reverberated into the living room. A moment later, Rebecca opened the kitchen door and came into the room. Twin blotches of color stained her cheeks, and her eyes held a distracted look.

She approached Emily and placed her hand on her daughter's flyaway curls. "The rain's stopped, sweetheart. Why don't you run over to the McClains and see if Lizzie wants to play."

With mischief gleaming in her eyes, Emily glanced down at her sock-clad feet. "Can I go barefoot?"

Rebecca shook her head. "I'll get your sneakers and help you put them on."

"What about Matt?"

"He's Dr. Tyler to you, young lady."

"Is he going to stay with us?"

"Dr. Tyler and I have to discuss that." Avoiding Matt's gaze, Rebecca disappeared into the hallway.

Emily cut her eyes toward Matt and rolled them with a sophistication far beyond her years. "That's why I have to play with Lizzie. So you and Mommy can talk."

Matt suppressed the urge to chuckle.

"I heard that," Rebecca's voice called from

deeper in the house.

She returned seconds later with a pair of tiny sneakers, placed them on Emily's feet and tied them snugly.

Emily hopped from the rocker. "See you later, Matt."

"Emily —" her mother warned.

Emily's gamine face crinkled in a grin. "I mean, Dr. Tyler."

"See you later, kid." The girl was a charmer, and he wondered if her mother would kick him out before the child returned.

After the front door closed behind Emily, Rebecca settled in the rocker her daughter had vacated, straightened her spine and looked him straight in the eye. "There's no easy way to put this, Dr. Tyler, so I'll just come right out with it. You can't stay here. I'm sorry."

He raised his hands, palms outward in apology. "I'm sorry if I've placed you in an awkward position."

"Dr. Peyseur placed you in one. I guess he didn't consider the consequences of a young single man as my houseguest."

Matt raised his eyebrows in disbelief. "That's the problem? We're in the twenty-first century, not the Dark Ages."

She shook her head, stirring the tumbled

41

mass of curls until he felt an irresistible urge to run his fingers through them. "Not in Warwick Mountain. We just left the eighteenth century during World War II, according to my grandmother."

He hadn't known a society filled with such restrictions existed in the United States. The standards Rebecca referred to were definitely foreign to the laid-back, anything-goes, weird-is-wonderful, always fluid culture of southern California that Matt had grown up in. "So my being 'Dr. Wonderful' isn't the problem?"

"It doesn't help," she admitted bluntly. "Every woman in the community read that magazine article about you at the beauty shop. And drew their own conclusions, whether the article was accurate or not."

Her voice ended on an upward note, like a question. The publicity piece had painted him as a superstud, or, as his mother might have said, a womanizer. Matt found Rebecca's interest in his social life flattering, until her next statement burst his bubble.

"I can't afford any question of my own reputation. As the local schoolteacher —"

"Caesar's wife?"

"Exactly. My own life must be above reproach or the people here won't want me teaching their children. There's a clause in my contract. Moral turpitude, I believe it's called."

He felt torn. On the one hand, he'd made his promise to Dwight and had also begun to look forward to knowing this forthright, unpretentious woman better. But on the other, if she kicked him out, he'd have the perfect excuse to take that cruise he needed so badly.

The choice should have been simple, but his conscience wasn't letting him off the hook that easily. He thought of all the families who needed his help, medical attention Dwight had been prepared to give until he'd broken his wrist. Matt had to make a stab at carrying out his friend's commitments.

"Isn't there somewhere else I can stay? Another family who might take me in?"

"Aunt Delilah and I went through the list of possibilities." She frowned with genuine disappointment. "None of them would work out. I'm sorry. Looks like you made this trip for nothing."

His conscience prodded him like a sharp stick. "What if I rented a motor home?"

Her face brightened an instant, then fell again. "There's still the question of where you'd park it. Keeping it here would raise the same red flags as your being a house-guest."

"There has to be someone —"

"The people of Warwick Mountain are poor but proud, with a long heritage of hospitality. No matter whose home you parked at, you'd put a strain on the people who live there."

"But I wouldn't need anything from them —"

"That's not the point. They would consider you their guest, and they would tax their own resources to provide you with electricity, water, meals —"

"I'd insist on paying."

She cocked her head and stared at him with that bright, open look he found so enticing. "You have a lot to learn about mountain folk. If you refuse their hospitality, you'll offend their pride. Offend one member of this community, and you'll offend them all, and the next thing you know, they'll refuse to accept treatment from you. They're touchy enough about accepting charity as it is. I'm sorry. I just don't see any way to make this work."

"We could get married," he said jokingly. "Then I could stay here without damaging your reputation."

At the mention of marriage, her expression closed, her entire demeanor stiffened, and he realized he'd hit a sore spot.

"Sorry," he said. "Guess that wasn't funny."

"Or helpful," she admitted, but added a hint of a smile as if to suggest he was forgiven.

"You really care about these people, don't you?"

She leaned toward him, her eyes sparking like green fire. "I grew up here. My parents died in a car accident when I was a baby, and Granny Warwick raised me. My neighbors are good people, salt of the earth. They'd share their last morsel of food and drop of water with you. If you need help with your chores, they'll pitch in to assist you before they do their own. This community is deeply rooted in two things — their traditional values and their love of the land. What they lack in money and worldly goods, they make up for in generosity and a zest for living."

He wanted her to keep talking, to watch the light flash in her eyes, the expressions scud across her face like clouds caught in the jet stream. "Tell me about the people Dwight planned to treat. I have his records in my briefcase, but I haven't had a chance to study them yet."

She relaxed against the back of the rocker and crossed her trim ankles. "Several of the farmers and their wives need skin cancers removed. They've worked all their lives in the outdoors. That exposure's taken its toll."

"Basal cell carcinoma or melanoma?" The first was bad enough, but the second could be fatal.

"We don't know. Dr. Peyseur intended to screen everyone."

"Anyone have a life-threatening illness?"

"Not that I'm aware of, although many of the men have been heavy smokers all their lives and probably should have their lungs checked. The most serious cases Dr. Peyseur planned to concentrate on are cosmetic."

Matt frowned. "From the way you've described your neighbors, I don't see them approving of cosmetic surgery."

Her laughter tumbled through the room like a mountain stream over rocks. "You mean like a face-lift? Not very likely." Her voice and expression sobered. "The worst case is Lizzie McClain."

"Where Emily went to play?"

Rebecca nodded. "Lizzie has a cleft lip and cleft palate."

"How old is she?"

"Almost ten."

Matt couldn't hide his shock. "Those defects are usually corrected before age one."

"Lizzie was born at home. I doubt she's seen a doctor a half dozen times in her life."

"You said she's the worst case. There're others?"

"Little Jimmy Dickens. He's eight and terribly scarred from burns when his mother accidentally scalded him with hot grease."

Matt winced. "Facial scars?"

"Face, neck, arms and hands. All highly visible. Jimmy's very self-conscious about them."

Memories of the society matrons and Hollywood celebrities who frequented his clinic complaining of encroaching wrinkles or bags beneath their eyes reproached him. Dwight, who'd been born in these hills, had felt drawn back to them later in life. No wonder he looked forward to this time in the mountains. His partner practiced medicine here that actually changed people's lives. Not that Matt would have that chance now. Rebecca Warwick had already made it perfectly clear that he couldn't stay.

The screen door at the front of the house slammed, and Matt heard giggles in the entryway.

"Emily," Rebecca called. "Is that you?"

Rebecca's back was to the hallway, but Matt could see the top half of a little girl's face as she peeked around the door frame. Coal-black hair framed an arresting pair of periwinkle-blue eyes dancing with curiosity. Emily stepped into the room and tugged the other child, an older girl, in with her. The newcomer kept her hand over her mouth and continued to stare at Matt with interest.

"That's Dr. Tyler," Emily said to the girl. "He's come to make you better." Rebecca's daughter turned to Matt. "Lizzie doesn't talk."

Can't talk, Matt reminded himself, at least not well without the roof of her mouth to help form the proper sounds. He gave the girl his warmest smile. "Then maybe she can just wave hello."

As he hoped, Lizzie took her right hand from her mouth and wiggled her fingers at Matt. Keeping his face from showing his distress at the severity of her disfigurement, the split in her upper lip that extended all the way to her nose, he waved back at her. "Hi, Lizzie. I'm glad to meet you. You're a very pretty girl."

He spoke the truth. Lizzie was a stunningly beautiful child, except for the cleft lip and palate, defects that his special skills could mend.

"Can we have some cookies, Mommy?" Emily asked.

Rebecca shook her head. "But there're fresh peaches in a bowl in the fridge."

"Can I show Lizzie the baby chicks?"

"Just be sure to keep the gate to the hen-house closed."

"See you later, Dr. Tyler," Emily said with a giggle and a friendly grin, and Lizzie waved again before following Emily into the kitchen.

Matt watched them go and temporarily thrust visions of a South Pacific paradise aside. If he went to work immediately and coordinated with the nearest surgery facility, two weeks were all he'd need to correct Lizzie's problem. He could leave the follow-up visits to a local doctor — removing the sutures, guarding against infection and scheduling speech therapy were tasks that almost any doctor could handle — and Matt would still have time for his Fiji cruise.

He turned to Rebecca. "I know you can't have me here, but I intend to stay and do Dwight's work, even if I have to sleep in my car in a field somewhere."

CHAPTER THREE

No wonder Matt Tyler had such a reputation with women. Becca failed to completely repress a wry grimace. Her own four-year-old daughter and ten-year-old Lizzie had gone gaga over the man, blushing and giggling when he turned on his charm. Was Becca the only woman in the house who hadn't fallen for him like a dead tree in a high wind?

She studied him closely, but couldn't tell whether Matt had been as touched by Lizzie's disfigurement as he appeared, or if he was merely a powerful, wealthy man used to having his own way. His motivations, however, changed nothing about the predicament she was in.

"Even if you slept in your car," she told him, "you'd still be considered the guest of the field's owner, so we're back to our original quandary."

He pushed to his feet and paced the

hearth in front of the fire. "Now that I've seen Lizzie, I can't just walk away without helping her. Isn't there an empty house or building I could rent for a few weeks?"

Becca felt the stirrings of admiration at his determination, but she squelched them quickly. Matt's concern with Lizzie didn't necessarily indicate compassion. For all Becca knew, the child merely posed a professional challenge.

"Every house in the area is occupied. Even some that are barely habitable," she said.

With a sigh of frustration, he rammed his hands into his pockets. "Surely there's somewhere I could stay and commute?"

"Not within forty mountain miles. We're one of the most isolated communities in western North Carolina."

"And nobody has an empty barn or shed where I could camp out?"

The solution to the problem popped into her head, and Becca wondered if her resistance to the doctor's charms had prevented her from thinking of it before. "The old feed store on Main Street is empty."

Matt's expression brightened. He jerked his hands from his pockets and rubbed them together. "That might work. Who owns it?"

"I do."

His surprise was evident. She didn't wonder. Sometimes the fact that she owned the property surprised even her. Especially when the mortgage payments came due. She and Emily had gone without to buy the old structure. Her car, actually Granny's car, was ten years old. They had no television satellite dish, no computer, and they'd had to postpone indefinitely Emily's dreams of a Disney World vacation to buy the old store. If Becca's plans for it materialized, though, every sacrifice would have been worth it.

"Is it livable?" Matt asked.

"Depends on what you mean by living." Becca considered the man with a critical eye. He'd probably never done without in his entire life. Aunt Delilah had said he had more money than God. His residential requirements would be more appropriately met by the staff and facilities of a Ritz-Carlton penthouse suite. The prospect of the wealthy, pampered doctor roughing it in the old store tugged her mouth into a smile. "It has a bathroom. Toilet and sink only, no tub or shower."

If the lack of bathing facilities fazed him, to his credit, he didn't show it. "A kitchen?" he asked.

She shook her head.

"I'd still like to check the place out, if that's all right with you."

She shrugged, figuring he'd take one look at the dusty old ruin and beat a fast retreat to California. "I'll see if Mrs. McClain will look after Emily."

A few minutes later, with the two girls settled under her neighbor's watchful eye, Becca climbed into the front seat of the Land Rover and took a deep breath. "I love that new-car smell. You were lucky to get a brand-new rental."

Matt turned the SUV around and headed down the mountain for the village. "It's not a rental. I bought it in Asheville."

Becca settled into the deep leather seat and fastened her seat belt. The car cost more than she earned in a year and had depreciated by thousands of dollars the minute he had driven it off the lot. She couldn't wrap her mind around having that kind of income to toss around. The doctor seemed to accept spending money as naturally as breathing.

So had Grady.

Her former fiancé had thought money could buy him anything. But she'd taught him differently, much to his — and his father's — surprise. She had refused to place a price on honor, dignity and self-respect. With a shudder of revulsion, she pushed those memories away and gazed out the window at the road ahead.

She always enjoyed the drive into the village. The rain had stopped, the clouds were lifting and the sun was shining. On the way down the mountain, every curve of the gravel road revealed breathtaking vistas of ridge after ridge of softly folded mountains clad in blue haze. These mountains were her home. She'd felt strangely exposed in the alien landscape when she'd gone to college at the edge of the North Carolina Piedmont in Chapel Hill, away from the Smokies' sheltering, comforting presence. She had always hungered to return to Warwick Mountain. She'd fled here when her world collapsed over five years ago, and she hadn't left since.

Didn't plan to. Ever.

Matt handled the hairpin curves smoothly, driving with the same easy confidence that seemed to suffuse every aspect of the man's personality. Becca wondered if his remarkable self-possession was the result of his incredible wealth or an innate characteristic. Nothing seemed to rattle the man. When confronted with a problem, he immediately looked for solutions — with the assumption they'd be there.

And solutions, she thought with a twinge of envy, were infinitely more available when money was also plentiful. Then she silently rebuked herself. Money couldn't buy love, and she wouldn't trade all of Dr. Wonderful's millions for her life on Warwick Mountain with Emily, family, friends and memories of Granny.

They passed orchards of gnarled apple trees, limbs heavy with ripening fruit; stands of ancient hickories and oaks with an understory of dogwoods and wild azaleas; and cultivated fields, hip high in corn, defying gravity to grow tall and straight on the steep forty-five-degree slopes.

"This is beautiful country," Matt said.

"Nice place to visit but you wouldn't want to live here?" Becca asked.

"What makes you say that?" Matt's tone implied curiosity rather than offense.

The Land Rover had rounded the last curve and exited the gravel secondary road onto the narrow blacktop of Warwick Mountain's Main Street. Actually, Warwick Mountain's only street.

"This isn't exactly Rodeo Drive." Becca pointed out the landmarks. "That's the Baptist church where the street dead-ends. Three houses on one side of the street, the feed store and convenience store/gas station on the other. You're not in California anymore, Toto."

Matt pulled in front of the feed store and parked. "I can tell that by the air."

Feeling her hackles rising in defense of her home territory, Becca turned on him. "What's that supposed to mean?"

The smile he flashed was one-hundred watt. "You can't see the air here. It's too clean. Unlike the smog I'm used to."

She bent her head to unfasten her seat belt, glad for the chance to avoid his face. As hard as she tried to dislike the man, he kept doing and saying things that won her over. Admiring her daughter, showing compassion for Lizzie, appreciating the quality of mountain air. Good thing he wouldn't be staying at her home. He'd probably have her eating out of his hand in no time, just like every other female on the planet.

Becca, however, had her experiences with Grady as a shield against the doctor's charms. She'd made a fool of herself over a man once.

Never again.

She opened the door and hopped to the curb. "Ready to inspect the real estate?"

Confident he'd take one look at the interior of the feed store and hop the first flight back to Los Angeles, she strode up the wooden stairs of the loading dock to unlock the wide, double front doors.

Matt watched her graceful ascent of the stairs with appreciation. Rebecca Warwick was like no other woman he'd ever met. In California, every female he'd encountered had been obviously impressed by his wealth and his status. He rarely had to ask a woman for a date. Someone always called him first, inviting him to this party or that opening. The enigmatic Miss Warwick was apparently totally unimpressed by his celebrity status or his money. Her only interest seemed to be helping the people of her community obtain medical care.

And protecting her reputation.

But hadn't she already damaged her standing in the community by having a child without a father? As conservative as she insisted her neighbors were, the people evidently didn't hold the circumstances of Emily's conception against Becca, or she wouldn't be teaching their children.

Questions swarmed him like mosquitoes on a summer night. Who was Emily's father and what had happened to him? Who could love such a vibrant woman and have such an adorable little girl and just walk away from them? Or maybe the man had died —

"Cold feet?" Rebecca stood at the top of the loading dock, looking down at him, and he realized he'd been lost in thought.

"We can forget this idea, if you like," she said. "I won't be offended if you decide you've already seen enough."

Matt turned his attention from the woman with the mocking green eyes to the ancient structure of the feed store. Taking the stairs two at a time, he joined her on the dock. "Too soon to make up my mind. I haven't seen anything yet. Lead the way."

With a flick of her delicate wrist, she keyed the rusty lock and disengaged it. The double doors swung open with a squeal of rusty hinges.

Rebecca grimaced at the noise.

"Nothing a little WD-40 can't fix," Matt assured her and followed her inside.

Late-afternoon sun spilled through the tall windows that ran the length of the building on both sides, and dust motes floated in the rays illuminating the huge timber-framed space. Marks on the floors, indicating where storage bins and displays had sat, and a few empty crates were the only items left in the building.

"Bathroom's at the rear." Becca nodded toward a closet-size enclosure in the back corner. "Otherwise, what you see is what you get."

Matt ran his hand along an exposed wall stud. "Good bones."

Rebecca looked puzzled. "That a medical term?"

"It's a building expression. The structure's well built with good materials. You can't find heart pine like this anymore."

"It may be well built, but I doubt it will suit you. As you can see —" she encompassed the open space and uncovered windows with a sweep of her hand "— there's no privacy, and definitely no creature comforts. Worse than living in a barn. At least in a barn, you'd have hay to sleep on."

"Trying to get rid of me?"

Although he'd made his tone joking, he couldn't help wondering why she seemed reluctant for him to stay. She'd certainly balked at all his other suggestions for boarding arrangements. Even though her reservations had sounded reasonable, he sensed her throwing up walls, as if afraid to allow him to get too close. Maybe her reaction was typical of someone who lived in such seclusion. Or maybe she just didn't want him upsetting her routine.

"Being realistic," she said. "If you don't rest well and eat well, you can't work. If you can't work, you're no help to anyone." She shrugged, lifting her shoulders in a manner that made him want to wrap his hands around them. "I knew this was a bad idea."

"Hold on." He strode toward the back of the building, stuck his head into the tiny bathroom, then paced off several feet of the adjoining space. "This can work."

She shook her head in exasperation. "How?"

"If you'll let me, I can frame and drywall a bedroom area —"

He stopped as her eyes widened in apparent disapproval.

"Or I could just string a few tarps for privacy —"

"You?" Skepticism dripped from the word.

"Sure. Why not?"

"You're a doctor, not a carpenter."

He enjoyed a smidgen of satisfaction. He'd apparently befuddled the unflappable Miss Warwick. "I'm a doctor and a carpenter."

Her puzzled look disappeared. "I get it. Woodworking is your hobby."

He shook his head. "More than a hobby. I'm a master carpenter."

Her bafflement returned. "Why?"

"Why not?"

"Afraid Hollywood's quest for eternal

youth will go bust and you'll need a backup career? I don't think so." She shook her head in disbelief.

"I haven't always been a plastic surgeon."

She tilted her head upward, at the same time lifting her lips in a smile so inviting he shoved his hands in his pockets to keep from reaching for her. "You mean you had a life before Dr. Wonderful?"

"You agreeable to letting me stay here?"

"If you're serious."

He nodded, then dragged a couple of abandoned fruit crates from a corner, dusted them off with his sleeve and set them in a rectangle of light pouring through a window. "Have a seat, and I'll bore you to death with the story of my life."

She glanced distrustfully at the crate, eased onto it, crossed her legs and clasped her hands around one knee. "Hope it's a short story."

"Short but not sweet." He settled on the crate across from her and wondered where the crazy impulse to tell all had come from. He never talked about his past. Never really even thought about it. But for some unfathomable reason, he wanted to share it with Rebecca Warwick.

"Don't tell me you were a bad little boy," she teased. "You must have had some discipline or you'd have never made it through medical school."

"I wasn't bad. Just poor."

She narrowed her eyes in disbelief. "The other kids drove a Mercedes or Porsche to high school and you only had a Toyota? That kind of poor?"

"Nope, the old-fashioned not-having-two-nickels-to-rub-together kind of poor. My father died when I was two. Killed by a drunk driver. No life insurance. My mother cleaned other people's houses to support us. I know what it's like to do without." He'd always felt ashamed of his past around his celebrity friends, but he felt no censure from Rebecca.

"That's why you became a doctor, so you wouldn't have to do without again?"

Her question shocked him, not by its bluntness — he'd come to expect that from her — but by triggering memories he hadn't thought of in years. "I went into medicine because I watched my mother sicken and die during my high-school years. I wanted to keep other children's mothers from dying before their time."

"So that's why you chose plastic surgery as a specialty?" She didn't try to hide the irony in voice.

"I chose plastic surgery because Dwight

adopted me as his protégé while I was in college. That's also where the carpentry came in."

He resisted the impulse to squirm under her gaze, knowing how shallow his words about his mother must have sounded. Somewhere along the line between her death and reaching the pinnacle of success, he'd lost sight of his original motivations. He pushed the uncomfortable realization away.

"I worked my way through college as a carpenter. I was framing an addition to Dr. Peyseur's Beverly Hills home when I first met him. He and Madeline sort of adopted me when they learned I had no family."

"Lucky you."

He heard the cynicism in her tone. "It wasn't what you think. Dwight didn't give me money. I was earning a good living, enough to pay my way, at least. What he gave me was encouragement — and a place where I felt I belonged."

"Beverly Hills." She raised a delicate eyebrow. "Must have been a very nice place to belong."

"It wasn't the place so much as the people. Dwight's like a father to me. And I miss Madeline almost as much as my own mother."

"Dwight's a good man. Emily and I had been looking forward to his visit."

"And now you're stuck with me instead."

"Not unless you choose to live here."

He glanced around the space again, picturing improvements in his mind. "It's doable."

"Question is," Rebecca said, "how much time for doctoring will you have if you're working to refurbish this place?"

He abandoned thoughts of Fiji temporarily, drawn by the prospect of working with wood, hammer and nails again. Maybe the physical exertion would do him as much good as a South Pacific cruise. It had been a long time since he'd worked up a sweat outside a gym or off a tennis court. Too long since he'd experienced the satisfaction of building something with his own hands.

Plastic surgery, of course, was construction, or reconstruction, but it was also stressful, with its intricacies and challenges, not to mention the expectations of his patients. Carpentry was good honest toil in the open air. And air didn't come any better than what he'd breathed on Warwick Mountain.

"I could have this place shaped up in three or four days," he estimated. "That includes framing in a temporary examination room and waiting area. Nothing I couldn't knock down in a hurry when I'm through here."

"No!" Rebecca jumped to her feet.

"Hey." Matt lifted his hands. "It was just a suggestion. I can just throw up tarps —"

"I meant don't tear down anything when you're through here. And I'll pay for the improvements."

"What if they don't suit your plans for this building? You plan to reopen the feed store?"

She shook her head. "Folks here would rather drive forty miles to pay discount prices at the big chain stores. I have other plans for this building."

She had tweaked his curiosity. "Turning it into a school?" he asked.

She sank back onto the crate. "So Dwight didn't tell you?"

"Is it a secret?"

She nodded. "No one knows but Dwight and me, just in case my idea doesn't work out. That way folks won't be disappointed."

He studied her with interest. Rebecca Warwick was blunt and direct, but she was far from simple. He sensed a depth to the woman quite different from the shallow starlets that moved in and out of his life like the tides on Malibu Beach.

"If you tell me what you're planning," he said, "I can build to your specifications."

65

She lifted her head to meet his gaze. "My grandmother would still be alive if we'd had an emergency clinic in Warwick Mountain. She died on the way to the Asheville hospital. Her heart gave out. The doctors there had the medicine that would have saved her, but she ran out of time before they could administer it."

"You plan to turn this place into an emergency clinic?" he asked in disbelief. He couldn't decide whether she was courageous or crazy. Maybe both.

She nodded. "I do."

Admiration swelled inside him, along with the knowledge that the spunky woman had bitten off more than she could chew. "A building's one thing. Do you have any idea how much it costs to furnish and staff the kind of clinic you're describing?"

She set her jaw in a stubborn line. "Dwight's helped me with the figures."

"Dwight encouraged this insanity?" he blurted. "He, of all people, should know what you're up against."

"He tried to talk me out of it at first." She tilted her chin at an angle, as if daring him to take a swipe at her. "But when he realized how serious I am, he said he'd help."

"Financing?"

She shook her head. "I didn't ask him for

money. I intend to apply for grants, appeal to charities. And I'm hoping when Dwight retires in a few years, he'll come here to supervise the clinic for us."

Matt let out a long, low whistle. "When you dream, girl, I have to give you credit, you dream big."

She threw her arms wide, encircling the space. "But my dream's coming true. I have the building. And now you've offered to build examining and waiting rooms. It's a start, anyway."

"Whoa," he warned her. "Don't get your hopes up. The improvements will be rough. If I'm treating patients, I won't have time for the finishing details." What was he getting himself into?

"Taking care of Lizzie and the others, that's the most important thing," Rebecca insisted.

Matt shoved to his feet. "Then I'd better get started. I'll take you back to your house, then head for the closest town for building supplies."

She scrutinized him with a stare that seemed to pierce right through him. "You're sure you want to do this?"

"Absolutely." And when he returned to California, he'd make an appointment with Ron Featherstone, the psychiatrist he played tennis with, to have his head examined.

He followed her outside, waited while she locked the double doors, then headed for the car.

He hoped he wasn't making a mistake. Rebecca's hopes for an emergency clinic in that old building were a pipe dream, as he'd already tried to tell her.

With a sigh, he took an internal reality check. Talk about pipe dreams. Building Becca's clinic wasn't Fiji, but it would definitely be a change.

CHAPTER FOUR

On the ride home, Becca argued with her conscience. Matt had given her the perfect out with his offer to head back to town for the materials he'd need. No need now to put him up in her house for even one night. But she couldn't be certain at this late hour that he'd be able to find accommodations, not at the height of the summer tourist season. And it was past suppertime.

She could almost hear Granny's voice, demanding to know what had happened to her manners. The man had come thousands of miles on an errand of mercy, had volunteered to begin building her long-hoped-for clinic, and she was willing to send him on his way without a hot meal or prospects for a bed to sleep in.

What was the matter with her?

Dr. Wonderful was the matter, that's what. She found the man entirely too charming, too likable, too agreeable. Too handsome, too rich, too —

The list seemed endless. And irrelevant. What difference did any of his attributes make? She wasn't interested. She didn't want, didn't need a man, any man, in her life. All that mattered was showing him the proper hospitality, especially in light of the sacrifices he was prepared to make to provide medical care to her neighbors.

"No need for you to head back to town tonight," she said. "It's getting late. You can stay with Emily and me."

"What will the school board think of that?" His voice seemed to hold genuine concern, as if the man really cared about her standing in the community.

She shook away the crazy thought. A man with a checkered reputation like his concerned about her reputation? Who was she kidding?

"Southern hospitality isn't a myth," she insisted. "We take our responsibilities to our guests very seriously."

"I don't want to cause problems."

"No problem." She hoped that was true. Surely she wouldn't be fired because of one overnight stay. "Besides, you'll need to measure the building before you order supplies. And I doubt you carry a tape measure in your medical bag."

"Are you offering to help?" Matt seemed surprised.

"If you need it. And you're welcome to borrow Grandpa's tools. His kit's in the barn."

He flicked his gaze toward her before returning his attention to the road, now deep in shadows with the sun dipping behind the mountain. "I wish I could at least take you and Emily out to dinner."

Rebecca laughed. "Eating out in Warwick Mountain means a moon pie and an RC Cola at the Shop-N-Go. Nothing like your fancy Beverly Hills restaurants. But thanks for the thought. I hope you don't mind leftovers."

"Leftovers were always my favorite, both my mom's and Madeline's. It's been ten years since I had any." He may have been just acting polite, but the wistfulness in his voice sounded genuine.

"Ten years without leftovers? What planet do you live on? Never mind, I know the answer. Planet Hollywood."

"The place isn't as weird as you make it sound." His attitude had turned defensive until he laughed. "Yes, it is. I stand corrected."

Becca squirmed. Granny would have been horrified at her rudeness. "I didn't mean to imply —"

"No offense taken. They don't call it la-la land for nothing." He pulled to the side of the road when they reached her house. "Okay to park out front or should I hide the car behind the barn in case someone passes by?"

He had to be teasing, for she could detect no malice in his question.

"Park out front. Let the neighbors know I have nothing to hide."

He threw her a glance that seemed to hold more than a hint of admiration, and killed the engine.

Becca climbed out. "I'll get supper started."

"Last chance," he said. "I'm still willing to spring for moon pies and RCs, if you'd rather not cook."

"Emily would take you up on that in a heartbeat, so do me a favor —" she nodded up the road where Emily was skipping toward home "— and don't tempt her."

"You're the mom." He reached behind him for his backpack, but not before flashing her a grin that made her knees weak. In spite of her best defenses, his charm was working its magic on her.

By the time he'd climbed out of the car, Emily had reached them. Her face lit up like a burst of fireworks when she saw Matt holding his backpack. "Are you staying, Dr. Matt?"

"Just for tonight," he said easily.

Her face drooped with disappointment. "Then you're going away?"

Matt shook his head and gave her daughter another smile so enchanting, Becca forced herself to look away. *Probably practices in front of the mirror,* she told herself, *perfecting the look that knocks starlets off their four-inch stiletto heels.*

"I've found another place to stay," Matt told Emily.

"Where?"

Becca noted that her daughter was so smitten with Matt, she had yet to acknowledge her mother's presence.

"You ask too many questions," Becca warned her. "Go wash up for supper."

"Yes, ma'am."

Emily skipped ahead of them into the house. Matt's gaze followed her, a softness on his face that almost made Becca reject her cynical assessment of him.

"She's a sweetheart," he noted.

"She can be hell on wheels at times, too," Becca admitted.

"Probably gets that from her mother." Brown eyes sparking devilishly, he opened the screen door for her with a flourish.

Unable to think of a snappy comeback, Becca breezed through the door, headed straight for the kitchen, then stopped.

Her guest had her so flustered, she'd forgotten her manners.

"Your room's this way." She headed down the hall and pointed to the doorway on the right. "Bedroom's here. Bath's across the hall. Come to the kitchen when you've had a chance to settle in."

"Not much settling needed for just one night," he said in a dry voice.

She was afraid to look at him, fearful that just seeing his handsome face would overwhelm her common sense. The man had to be aware he oozed appeal. Especially in the narrow confines of the hallway — in front of Granny's room.

The thought of her grandmother calmed Becca's galloping pulse and allowed her to ignore the glimmer in his eyes.

She took a deep breath to steady herself. "Supper in ten minutes."

She pivoted and fled to the kitchen.

She yanked leftovers from the refrigerator, turned on the stove beneath the pot of black-eyed peas, shoved a dish of collard greens into the microwave to heat and began making biscuits.

Emily, face still damp from scrubbing, came in and climbed onto the stool beside the counter where Becca rolled out dough.

"You mad, Mommy?"

"Of course not, sweetie," she lied. She was mad, though — at herself. How could she allow Matt Tyler to affect her, especially after all the painful lessons her attraction to Grady had taught her? "What makes you say that?"

"Your face looks mad."

Becca forced her expression to relax and vowed not to take her frustrations out on her daughter. "I'm just in a hurry. Will you put the butter on the table, please?"

Minutes later, Matt appeared on the threshold. Becca tried not to notice how fantastic he looked, his tall frame almost filling the door, his head scant inches from the lintel.

"What's that incredible smell?" he asked.

"Mommy's baking biscuits," Emily said.

He inhaled deeply with obvious appreciation, then stepped into the room. "*Homemade* biscuits? Rebecca Warwick, will you marry me?"

As hard as she fought against it, she found his humor infectious.

"Cheaper to hire a cook," she said with a laugh. "Besides, don't go jumping to conclusions. You haven't tasted my cooking yet."

She motioned him to a chair at the table, and he settled beside Emily. She placed the dish of black-eyed peas between the platter of sugar-cured ham and the bowl of collard greens and added a relish dish filled with Granny's chowchow, the last she'd canned before she died. "Help yourself."

He didn't need a second invitation and began filling his plate as if he hadn't eaten for a week. "If everything tastes half as good as it smells, I'll stand by my original offer."

"If you marry Mommy," Emily said, "would that make you my daddy?"

Matt spread butter on a hot biscuit. "That's right." He took a bite of biscuit and closed his eyes as if in a trance. "Best biscuit I ever tasted."

"You'd make a nice daddy," Emily said.

"Emily!" Becca slid into her place at the table. "Matt is only kidding."

"Oh." The little girl's expression relayed her disappointment. "But I want a daddy. Everybody else has one."

Becca felt a spasm of guilt, but this was not a conversation to have with Emily in front of a stranger.

"Not everybody has a daddy," Matt said with a gentleness that scored more points with Becca. "My daddy died when I was younger than you are now, and my mother and I got along fine, just the two of us, like you and your mother."

Emily set her fork down and gazed at her mother. "Did my daddy die?"

Matt flicked his eyes toward Becca, obviously curious, but she wouldn't be forced into a discussion Emily wasn't ready for. The subject was too complex for a four-and-a-half-year-old's comprehension.

"What did you and Lizzie do this afternoon?" she asked.

"Watched Mrs. McClain peel peaches."

Matt cocked an eyebrow and grinned at Becca. "Is that the local equivalent of watching paint dry?"

"It's canning time," she explained. "She's getting ready to put up preserves."

"Miss Habersham came to visit her," Emily added. "They talked a lot."

"I don't doubt it. The Habersham sisters are our resident gossips," Becca explained to Matt. "Warwick Mountain doesn't need a newspaper. Everyone hears all they need to know from one of the Habershams."

"One?" Matt helped himself to more ham from the platter she passed him and slid a slice inside a biscuit. "How many are there?"

"Four," Becca explained. "None of the sisters ever married. The oldest is ninety-eight, the youngest eighty-three. They still live on the homestead their great-grandparents built."

"Alone?" Matt asked.

Becca nodded. "Uncle Jake's nephew helps with their livestock, but they grow their own garden, fix their own meals. They're very independent."

"Mommy," Emily asked, "what's a playboy?"

"Where did you hear a word like that?" Becca asked.

"Miss Habersham said Dr. Matt's a playboy," the girl said. "Is that a bad word?"

Becca noted that Matt had the grace to look uncomfortable. She couldn't resist tossing the ball into his court. "No, it's not a bad word. Tell her what it means, Matt."

"Me?" Matt almost choked on his biscuit.

"Makes sense," Becca said with her sweetest smile as she planted her barb. "Don't you have firsthand experience?"

Matt swallowed hard and turned to Emily. "A playboy is a man who has so much money he doesn't need to work for a living, so he spends all his time doing the things he enjoys."

Emily cocked her head and considered his definition. "That's not what Miss Habersham said."

"What did Miss Habersham say?" Matt ignored Becca's attempts to shush him.

Emily scrunched her face as if trying to remember. "A playboy is a man who has more money than he has sense."

"Is that what she said about me?" Matt said.

Emily nodded. "She said she read it in a magazine."

Becca couldn't resist throwing him an I-told-you-so look. "Guess everyone's read about Dr. Wonderful."

Emily apparently wasn't going to let the subject drop. "Do you have more money than sense, Dr. Matt?"

Matt glanced at Becca with a plea for help. "How do I answer that?"

"Honestly?" Becca suggested, then took pity on him. "Emily, it's not polite to ask people how much money they have."

"Or how much sense?" the girl asked.

"That's not polite, either," her mother said.

"Then why did Miss Habersham talk about it?" Emily asked. "I thought grown-ups were always polite."

"Are you sure this kid's only four and a half?" Matt said. "Sounds like she'd make a great attorney."

Becca sighed. "I have to admit, she's good

at cross-examination."

"Miss Habersham said you have lots of girlfriends," Emily continued. "Is Mommy one of them?"

"Who wants to know?" Becca asked with alarm. "You or Miss Habersham?"

"Me," Emily said. "Miss Habersham didn't say anything about you, Mommy."

Becca breathed a sigh of relief. Once the Habershams started a rumor, it blazed through the community like wildfire in dry grass with a high wind behind it.

"Your mother's a girl and she's my friend," Matt said. "And so are you."

"I am?" Emily said with a touch of awe.

"Sure." Matt had handled the girlfriend issue with an ease that won Becca's reluctant respect. "You're Dr. Dwight's girlfriends, too. That's why he sent you presents."

"Can I have mine now?" Emily asked.

"Not until after supper," Becca said. "Finish your peas, and I'll serve Aunt Delilah's chocolate pound cake."

"With ice cream?" Emily asked.

Becca nodded.

Matt wiped his mouth with his napkin and sighed with satisfaction. "Best meal I ever tasted. There's a little bistro in Westwood claims to serve Southern food, but it can't touch this."

"It's the mountain air," Becca said. "Visitors often say it improves the appetite."

Matt looked longingly at the solitary biscuit left in the bread basket, even though he'd already had three. "Nope. Has to be the cooking. My offer of marriage still stands."

The twinkle in his eye was almost irresistible, but Becca somehow managed to avoid melting to his charm. She stood and began to clear the plates. "Maybe it'd be easier if I just teach you to make biscuits."

"Can I watch?" Emily asked.

"Ready to see a grown man make a fool of himself?" Matt said.

"Dr. Matt?" the girl said.

"Yes?"

"Is a playboy a bad man?"

"Not necessarily."

Emily frowned. "Mrs. McClain said no playboy was going to touch her Lizzie."

Matt stifled a sigh and Becca's heart dropped. "Are you sure you heard right, Emily?"

The girl nodded. "And Miss Habersham agreed with her."

"You mustn't repeat that to anyone," Becca said. "I'm sure once Mrs. McClain meets Dr. Tyler, she'll be happy to have him treat Lizzie."

Emily turned to Matt. "Are you going to make Lizzie pretty?"

"Lizzie's already pretty. I'm just going to fix her lip and mouth so she can talk as well as other people." He lifted his head and met Becca's gaze across the kitchen. She saw her own worry reflected in his eyes. "If Mrs. McClain will let me," he added.

Later, Matt sat in a rocker on the front porch, watching tiny lights dart and flicker across the front yard.

"Lightning bugs." Rebecca came out of the house, handed him a mug of coffee and sat in the rocker next to him.

"Same as fireflies?" Matt asked.

Rebecca nodded.

Matt felt relaxed and comfortable in her company. He tried to pinpoint the quality that made her unique. Wholesomeness? He mentally rejected that. Although she glowed with health and projected a sense of being at ease with herself, that wasn't what caught his attention. Something made her different from other women he'd known.

Naturalness.

That was it. When he looked at Rebecca, he saw the real article, nothing fake, contrived or affected.

"Emily asleep?" he asked.

Rebecca nodded again and sipped her coffee. "Finally. She's been all wound up today. Took her a while to settle down."

"She's a sharp little girl. Pretty, too."

"Thanks," she said, but her tone was distracted. "At least she's warned us what we're up against."

"Mrs. McClain?"

"I can't believe the woman said that. Ever since I first suggested the surgery for Lizzie, she's been excited about it."

"That was when Dwight was handling it."

Rebecca shrugged. "That's true. The McClains know Dwight, and they trust him."

"Maybe I can get them to trust me, too."

Rebecca stopped the gentle action of her rocker. "That could take a while. Folks here are hospitable, but they're slow to accept strangers."

"And I'm Dr. Wonderful, about as strange as they come." Resentment stirred in him. He'd never expected his lifestyle to interfere with his treatment of a patient, had never even considered the possibility. And it had been years since he'd felt as strong a desire to heal as he had when he met Lizzie McClain.

"Give them time," Rebecca suggested.

Matt bit back his reply. He'd planned on

performing Lizzie's surgery quickly and then having a little time left for his vacation. Dwight had, however, warned him nothing moved quickly in this region.

"Mountain time," the old doctor had called it, and he hadn't been referring to the time zone. "People move at their own speed," Dwight had said, "and usually it's slow or slower."

"That would drive me nuts," Matt had answered.

"Actually, you get used to it. Sometimes, especially when I'm stuck on the freeway, I long for it."

With the soothing rustle of the breeze in the trees, the gentle motion of his chair, the lack of the distracting blare from a television and the bothersome rumbling of traffic, Matt had to admit there was something hypnotic about the mountain atmosphere that unraveled the tension in a man's muscles as effectively as a massage.

Or maybe the woman beside him had something to do with how he felt.

He'd surprised himself earlier by his impromptu proposal of marriage. Although he'd asked in jest, the idea had taken root with a certain allure that he couldn't shake. Despite the hundreds of beautiful women he'd treated in his practice or partied with in Hollywood and Malibu, the prospect of marriage to any one of them had never crossed his mind.

He'd already determined that Rebecca's natural manner made her different from the others. But there was more than that. Maybe it was her complete indifference to him as a man. Had he taken her attitude as a challenge? Maybe if she showed some interest in him personally, her appeal would lessen.

The silence on the mountain was deafening. Only the slightest ruffling of leaves and the muted creak of the rockers broke the stillness. If he stayed here long, Matt thought, he'd soon go into withdrawal, longing for the sixty channels on his wide-screen television or a quick drive to Sunset Strip for some delicious food at The Standard.

"What do people do around here for entertainment?" he asked.

She looked at him askance. "Most folks work so hard, by nightfall or on Sunday, they're happy to sit on their porches and relax."

"I saw a television in your living room. You and Emily ever watch it?"

"The mountains usually block reception. Sometimes, if weather conditions are right, we can tune in the Asheville stations, but we don't count on it." She drank more of her coffee. "Besides, Emily would rather hear stories."

"You read to her?" A pleasant childhood recollection of sitting on his mother's lap as she read to him flashed through his mind, something he hadn't thought about in years.

"We don't get our stories from books. Storytelling is a family tradition. No one could tell a story like my granny, but I try to fill the void and keep the oral tradition going. I hope one day Emily will tell these stories to her children."

"Tell me a story." He surprised himself with the suggestion, but he enjoyed the slow, soft drawl of her voice and wouldn't mind listening to more.

"What kind would you like to hear?"

He'd expected her to be coy, to want to be begged to perform, but she hadn't hesitated.

"What are my choices?" he asked.

"Humorous stories, stories that teach a lesson, like in ethics or history, ghost stories —"

"I don't believe in ghosts."

"You would if you lived in these mountains for a while." Her smile was challenging. "People have written entire books on Tarheel ghosts. And ghost stories are Emily's favorites."

"Okay, I'm game." He settled deeper into his chair. "Let's see if you can make a believer out of me."

She straightened her back and cleared her throat. "Back at the turn of the century, in a small town on the other side of Asheville, a farmer built a new home for his family." Her voice had deepened and taken on a more serious tone. "The day they moved into the new house was a long and happy one, and that night, long after his usual bedtime, the farmer sat in the front parlor, reveling in his new domain before turning in.

"He wound the mantel clock and set the time, noting it was almost midnight, the time the nightly freight train passed down in the valley on its regular run. Still too excited to sleep, the farmer lit his pipe and returned to his chair by the fire.

"As the clock struck midnight, the farmer could hear the whistle of the passing train. To his amazement, the front door that he had locked and bolted earlier swung open as if pushed by an invisible hand."

An owl hooted eerily in a nearby tree, as if right on cue, and the temperature of the breeze dropped a few degrees, raising goose bumps on Matt's arms. He had to give her credit. Her delivery was perfection, better than any of the actresses he'd dated.

"The farmer jumped from his chair," Rebecca continued in a dramatic tone, "and hurried to check the door. His entire family was asleep. No one else had been in the room, nor could he find a sign of anyone on the porch or near the house. Perplexed, the farmer locked the door again and went to bed.

"The second night he retired at his usual time, making certain to lock the front door securely. But when he awoke the next morning, the door stood open. In the weeks that followed, the farmer, members of his family and even some of his neighbors sat up until midnight. All observed the same phenomenon. When the midnight freight passed, the door swung wide as if opened by some ghostly hand."

Matt smiled to himself. He'd already figured out where the story was going. The door's opening had a scientific explanation, and he wondered why Rebecca had chosen this particular tale to convince him of the existence of ghosts.

"Now, the farmer was an intelligent man," Rebecca said, "and didn't believe in spirits. He knew there had to be a practical reason for the door that opened itself. So he wrote to the university at Cullowhee and asked if scientists could study the site.

"Within weeks, several geologists had analyzed the ground beneath the farmer's house and concluded that the same bedrock under the house ran into the valley beneath the train tracks. They concluded the rumblings from the train traveled through the rock, setting up vibrations that caused the door to swing open on its own."

Feeling smug that he'd been right, Matt waited for the ending.

"Happy that he'd solved the mystery of the self-opening door, the farmer thought no more about it, other than to make a point of closing the door each morning when he awoke. Months later, however, he was up late with a sick cow. Passing through the living room on his way to bed, he noticed the time was almost midnight. He could set his watch by the train whistle. But as the clock struck twelve, not a sound issued from the valley below. As the last chime died away, however, the front door creaked on its hinges and swung open.

"The next day, the farmer learned that the midnight freight had been delayed by a rock slide on the other side of the mountain — but his door had opened, nonetheless. No longer skeptical about the presence of a ghost in his house, he put the place up for sale and moved his family to another mountain.

"The next family didn't stay long in that house, either, and soon the house was abandoned, its reputation too well known for anyone to dare living there. Years later, the midnight freight run was canceled, but even today, for those who are brave enough to visit the decrepit house, someone — or something — opens the door at midnight."

She sat back and laced her hands around her now-empty coffee cup.

"A great story," he conceded, "but you made it up, right?"

She smiled and shook her head. "The phenomenon's been documented."

Her response startled him, and he wouldn't have believed it, except for the fact that Rebecca seemed too much of a straight shooter to lie. "And there's no explanation?"

Her enticing smile widened. "Not unless you believe in ghosts."

He couldn't decide whether she was teasing or serious and was surprised when she rose from her chair and wished him goodnight. It wasn't yet ten o'clock, far too early for his usual bedtime, even factoring in jet lag.

"Pleasant dreams," she said with a hint of teasing.

"Any resident ghosts I should know about?" he asked.

"Only Granny, but she won't hurt you." She slipped inside the house, and again, he didn't know if she'd been serious or pulling his leg.

He rose and followed her inside, where she started up the stairs. "Rebecca, aren't you going to lock the door?"

She paused and turned. "You can, if it makes you feel safer. No one in Warwick Mountain locks doors. Crime isn't a problem here." Her green eyes twinkled. "And locks don't keep the ghosts out."

Recalling the state-of-the-art security system in his Malibu home, he shook his head, feeling as if he'd traveled either back in time or to a foreign land.

Rebecca started back up the stairs, then stopped again. "By the way, please call me Becca. Everyone else does."

"Sure." The name suited her. Unpretentious and to the point. "Good night, Becca."

Maybe he'd allowed his affection for her to show in his voice, because a flush started at the base of her throat and worked its way to her cheeks. "Good night, Matt."

She almost ran up the stairs and disappeared around the landing without a backward glance.

Matt, feeling suddenly lonely, entered the guest room and stripped off his clothes. Although the room was snug and attractively furnished with antiques and country quilts, and the bed comfortable with sheets fragrant with fresh air and sunshine, he feared he'd toss and turn for hours. Surprisingly, he drifted almost instantly into a deep sleep.

Until an icy hand caressed his cheek and jerked him wide awake.

Chapter Five

Startled, disoriented, and remembering Becca's warnings of Granny Warwick's ghost, Matt bolted upright and gazed around the room, seeing no one in the pale moonlight that streamed through the windows and dimly lit the space. The fluorescent dial on the bedside clock read twenty minutes past midnight.

"Dr. Matt," a shaking voice whispered beside the bed. "It's me, Emily."

Matt spotted the girl, whose head barely reached the top of the high bed. "What are you doing up in the middle of the night?"

He reached for the lamp on the bedside table.

"No!" She grabbed his hand. "No lights! You'll scare them."

Her hand was freezing, and he could feel her shivering. In the faint light, he could barely make out her thin cotton Scooby Doo pajamas. He grabbed the extra blanket at the foot of his bed and flung it around her.

"Is something wrong?" He wondered why the child hadn't gone to her mother. "Is your mother all right?"

"She's asleep," Emily said.

Matt thought longingly of the deep, peaceful sleep she'd disturbed. "Then why did you wake me?"

"So you can see the ghosts. Lizzie won't believe me. But she will if you see them."

Matt shook his head in an attempt to clear the dregs of sleep. The entire Warwick family was obsessed with ghosts. "Ghosts don't exist except in stories."

"They're in the woods behind the house. I saw them. Come see."

Taking a look and proving nothing was there would be the only way to dissuade her and send her back to bed. "Wait for me in the hall. I'll be there in a minute."

Once Emily had left, he jumped from the bed, shivered in the frigid air and quickly pulled on his pants and shirt. Barefoot, he joined Emily in the hall. "Now, where are these so-called ghosts?"

Clasping the blanket around her with one hand, she grabbed his hand with her other and headed for the kitchen. When she tripped over the blanket, he caught her

before she fell, then scooped her in his arms
and carried her.

"We can see from the back porch." She
twined her tiny arms around his neck and
laid her head on his shoulder with a trust
that touched him. He'd never held a child
before, hadn't realized how sweet one
smelled, how fragile one felt. For the first
time, he wondered what holding a child of
his own might be like.

Matt carried her through the kitchen,
stepped out the back door and stopped
short. Deep in the woods far behind the
house, two lights bobbed up and down
through the trees, then stopped, hanging as
if suspended in space.

"See," Emily whispered in his ear. "I told
you."

"I see," Matt whispered back, "but they're
just lights. Somebody's carrying them, but
that doesn't mean they're ghosts."

"Somebody want to tell me what's going
on?" Becca's voice demanded behind them,
shattering the stillness and echoing across
the yard.

In the woods, the lights went out.

"Emily and I were looking at the strange
lights," Matt said.

"What lights?" Suspicion put an edge to
Becca's voice.

"Ghosts were in the woods, Mommy, but you scared them away."

"Come inside before you freeze to death," Becca said. "Both of you."

Following Becca, Matt carried Emily into the kitchen. Becca closed the door behind them and snapped on the light. Matt blinked at the sudden brightness, then blinked again at the sight of Becca in sweatpants, socks and an oversize T-shirt, her hair tousled from sleep, her cheeks pink with alarm and her green eyes narrowed in contemplation.

A strong surge of protectiveness swept through him, and startled him. He'd never had that response to a woman before — except for his mother in the last stages of her illness. Becca Warwick was a paradoxical mix of self-confidence and vulnerability. She carried herself with a defiant lift of her perfectly shaped chin, as if life had knocked her off her feet once, and she dared it now to take a swipe at her again.

"Emily woke me up and asked me to look at the lights." His emotions left him strangely tongue-tied, feeling almost guilty, like a little boy who'd been caught with his hand in the cookie jar. "I didn't want her leaving the house alone, not if someone was out there."

"Was anyone there?" Becca asked. "I

didn't see anything."

"There was lights, Mommy. Ghosts."

"There were lights," Matt agreed, "but I couldn't tell what they were. Does someone live back there?"

Becca shook her head, and a frown creased the smooth skin between her eyebrows. "It's all woods for miles."

"See," Emily said with an emphatic nod, "I told you they were ghosts."

"I doubt that, young lady." Becca reached for her daughter and Matt handed the girl over. His hand brushed Becca's, warm and soft.

"Probably hunters after coons," Becca told Emily. "I'm putting you to bed."

Becca gathered her daughter close, then turned to Matt, her expression softening. "Thanks for looking out for her."

"My pleasure," Matt said, surprised to realize it really had been.

"Will you turn out the light?" Becca asked.

Matt nodded, waited until they'd reached the stairs in the hall, then switched off the light.

As he crawled between the cold sheets in the guest room, he wondered what it would be like to be the man in charge of looking after Emily and Becca on a daily basis — for real.

The thought kept him awake for most of the night.

Becca couldn't drift back to sleep. She kept picturing Matt with Emily in his arms, and the scene filled her with guilt. For years, she and Emily had done fine, first with Granny, then just the two of them. But seeing Matt holding Emily tonight had brought home with a vengeance the fact that her daughter had no significant male figure in her life.

Sure, there was Uncle Jake, but he was such a crusty old codger, he sometimes frightened the little girl. Her heart ached over Emily's comments at supper about wanting a daddy. But Becca could think of no way to explain to a four-year-old that her father hadn't wanted her or her mother.

Trying to find a comfortable position, she turned on her stomach and punched her pillow. This was all Matt Tyler's fault. Emily hadn't said anything about daddies until the doctor had arrived. And Becca hadn't felt the stirrings of dissatisfaction, the sense that something was missing from her life until the too-handsome Dr. Wonderful had shown up at her door.

She slugged her pillow again. She didn't need a man to make her happy. She'd been perfectly content with Emily and teaching at the one-room schoolhouse. So why did she ache now for something she couldn't name?

The quicker she could move Matt out of her house in the morning, the better. Then her association with him would be limited to introducing him to his potential patients. After that she could forget he existed.

But right now, he was in the room below hers, his rugged good looks and easy charm enough to make any woman restless.

Becca took a deep breath. Grady had had that effect on her and look where she'd landed. She wouldn't trade anything in the world for Emily, but she'd learned a valuable lesson. Never again would she risk such heartache and humiliation. No matter how much she yearned for Dr. Wonderful, her brain knew he was a playboy who would never commit, never leave the luxurious and exotic Beverly Hills for the hardscrabble mountain life. Any relationship with him would be temporary.

And disastrous.

Even after resolving the issue, however, she took over an hour to fall asleep.

Emily was still sleeping when Becca tiptoed down the stairs at dawn the next morning, and the door to Matt's room was closed.

She was looking forward to a peaceful cup of coffee alone while she mulled over the best way to approach the McClains about agreeing to authorize Lizzie's treatment.

Before she reached the kitchen, a forceful knocking sounded at the front door. When she opened it, three of the four Habersham sisters stood on her front porch. With their large bright eyes, fragile bones and brightly colored dresses, they looked like a trio of colorful sparrows.

"We've come to see the doctor," Hettie, ninety-one and the next to the eldest, said. "We know he's here. That's his car, isn't it? Here awful early, isn't he? 'Less he spent the night?"

"Come in." Becca ignored Hettie's question, swung the door wide and ushered them into the living room out of the early-morning mist that swirled on the porch. She had already noted that Grace, the eldest, wasn't with them. "Is Grace ill?"

"Her rheumatism's acting up," Fannie, the youngest at eighty-three, announced, "so she didn't feel up to the walk down the mountain this morning. But she'll be right as rain when the weather dries out."

"But you want to see the doctor?" Becca asked, puzzled.

"Oh, yes," Sophie's blue eyes shone with

excitement. "We've never met a celebrity before."

"Unless you count that man at the supermarket in town," Fannie said. "The one that made all those toilet-paper commercials."

Becca suppressed the urge to roll her eyes. "I'm afraid the doctor's still asleep —" There, she'd said it. The wily sisters probably already knew he'd spent the night.

"Not anymore," Matt's deep, husky voice announced behind her.

The three elderly sisters collectively caught their breaths.

"Oh, my," Hettie said. "You're even more handsome than your pictures."

"And so tall," Fannie said appreciatively.

"We wouldn't have bothered you this early," Sophie said, "but we heard you were going back to California, and we didn't want to miss you. Since this would be our only chance to see you, we brought you breakfast."

She held up a basket, its contents wrapped in a red-and-white checkered linen napkin. "Fresh-baked buttermilk biscuits."

Hettie held up a jar of golden liquid. "With sourwood honey from our own bees."

"Or mayhaw jelly, if you'd rather," Fannie said, holding up another glass jar. "I made it myself."

"That's very kind of you, ladies." Matt's voice was gracious, but Becca took delight in watching him squirm beneath the elderly sisters' scrutiny as he accepted their gifts.

"What makes you think the doctor's leaving?" Becca asked.

"You know how it is on the mountain," Hettie said evasively. "Word gets around."

"That particular rumor's wrong," Becca told them. "Dr. Tyler will be here for several weeks."

"He's staying *here*?" Fannie asked, and shock registered on the three elderly faces.

"He's made other arrangements." Becca refused to satisfy their obvious curiosity. "He can't leave Warwick Mountain yet. He has patients to treat."

She didn't miss the questioning glance exchanged between the three. They were dying to know Matt's plans, but Becca kept quiet.

"If I can be of help to any of you," Matt offered, juggling the basket and jars that filled his hands, "let me know."

"Oh, we're as healthy as horses," Fannie insisted a bit too quickly. "Never had a sick day in our lives — except for Grace's rheumatism. But she has her own remedy for that."

Becca repressed a grin. Grace's remedy

was home-brewed and one-hundred-fifty proof. One dose and Grace felt no pain.

"Is it true," Sophie asked Matt, "that you're keeping company with Anna Lisa Patton?"

"Keeping company?" Matt said with a puzzled frown.

"Hooking up," Becca translated. "Hanging out."

She waited, interested in his reply. Anna Lisa was Hollywood's sexiest young actress with a line of rejected lovers that would reach from Warwick Mountain to the West Coast.

Matt cleared his throat, as if stalling for time. "I've, uh, spent some time with Anna Lisa," he said with unsatisfying vagueness, making Becca wonder what his involvement with the blond bad girl had been.

Hettie sighed. "She was beautiful in *Midnight Seduction*."

"You saw that movie?" Becca blurted in surprise. The spinster sisters were the last she'd have expected to view the raciest film out of Hollywood in the last five years.

"Heavens, no," Hettie said with a laugh. "I read about it in a magazine. We haven't been to the picture show since 1939 when Papa took us to Asheville to see *Gone with the Wind*."

Fannie giggled. "He herded us out before the show was over. Almost had apoplexy when Clark Gable said, 'Frankly, my dear, I don't give a —' "

"Fannie!" Hettie cut her off. "Watch your language. And your memory's slipping."

"That's right," Sophie said. "We went with the church group in 1964 to see *The Sound of Music.*"

"That's right," Fannie said. "Julie Andrews was so pretty, especially in the wedding scene where she married Captain Von Trapp. What a beautiful dress. And the music . . ." She sighed heavily, remembering.

Becca felt a pang of sympathy for Matt, who stood listening to the nonstop talkers, probably wondering how he could escape.

"Have you met Julie Andrews?" Fannie asked him.

Matt nodded. "She's a lovely, gracious lady. But I don't keep company with her," he added quickly.

The three sisters tittered as if Matt had said the funniest line they'd ever heard, and Becca took the opportunity to herd them toward the front door. "Thank you for stopping in, but I'm sure you're anxious to check on Grace. And you don't want Dr. Tyler's biscuits to get cold."

"Goodbye, ladies," Matt called behind her. "Thanks again for bringing breakfast."

Relieved to be rid of the talkative trio, Becca closed the front door after them and hurried back to the living room. She took the basket of biscuits from Matt and headed toward the kitchen. He followed with the jelly and honey.

"Do they always talk that much?" Matt set the jars on the table. "I feel shell-shocked."

"They were just getting warmed up. I was lucky to get them out of here so quickly. Sometimes they settle in for half a day." Becca filled the coffeemaker with fresh grounds and water and flipped the switch. "By noon today, everyone within five miles will know you spent the night here."

"I should have returned to town."

"I wasn't complaining," she said hastily. "Just demonstrating the efficiency of their mass-communication system."

"You should have asked them about last night," Matt said.

"Last night?"

"The lights in the woods. If they know everything that goes on around here, maybe they know what the lights were."

Becca frowned. "I've never seen lights there before."

"Thought you said it was hunters."

"Did you hear dogs?"

"There was no sound, just lights."

"Coon hunters would have had dogs with them."

"Maybe it was car headlights from a highway."

She shook her head. "Our land takes up forty acres behind the house. Past that is national forest. No roads."

"Hiking trails?"

"Not in that part of the forest. Beyond our land the terrain's rugged, filled with deep ravines. More suited for rock climbing than hiking."

"You don't believe ghosts caused the lights?" His brown eyes were mocking, and he looked entirely too appealing dressed in a beige fisherman's sweater and jeans.

"I have no idea. Folks swear the Brown Mountain lights are caused by ghosts. Stranger things have happened in these mountains."

"Doesn't it worry you, not knowing who was out there or why?"

"The only thing that worries me is that the lights were extinguished when I spoke loud enough for whoever it was to hear. That indicates that whoever was out there had a reason to hide."

He cast a covetous look at the basket of biscuits, then glanced back to her. "Want to take a look?"

"At what?" She blushed, realizing she'd been staring at him, appreciating the attractiveness that had placed him on the cover of *People.*

"At the woods where the lights were. Maybe there'll be tracks or some other clue to what was out there."

Going outside seemed like a good idea. The cozy intimacy of being in the kitchen with Dr. Wonderful was a bit much, and the cool morning air would clear her head.

"Okay." She reached for her jacket on a peg by the back door.

"What about Emily?" Matt asked.

"She's still asleep. I'll leave the door open, so she'll know we're out back. Sound travels in the mountains. We'll hear if she calls us."

Becca stepped onto the porch and hurried down the stairs to the gravel path that led past the barn, chicken coop and vegetable garden to the large open meadow between the house and the woods.

"Wow," Matt said behind her. "Did you plant these?"

Becca turned to catch him staring at the field in amazement. The sun had crested the ridge and reflected in the dew sparkling on the lush green grasses and the flashy yellow of the black-eyed Susans and brilliant white of the Queen Anne's lace.

A man who appreciated the beauty of nature couldn't be a total jerk, but she didn't want to think about Matt's redeeming qualities. She wanted reasons to resist his charm, as she was having a difficult time doing just that.

"They're wildflowers," she explained. "Granny used to graze horses and cattle here, but we haven't had livestock, except for chickens, in years."

She pressed ahead through the thigh-high grass. Matt walked beside her.

"Should you be watching for snakes?" he asked.

She felt a thrill of satisfaction at the concern for her in his voice, but quickly tamped it down. Plastic surgeon to the stars, she reminded herself, with a roving eye and probably the thickest little black book in Hollywood. "If I make enough noise and motion, they'll get out of my way."

"Do you own a gun?"

She stopped and looked at him. The man was definitely out of his element. "For snakes?"

He nodded toward the woods where he'd said the lights had been. "For protection."

It had been a long time since anyone had shown such concern for her welfare, but the pleasure his caring gave her was dangerous, and weakened the walls that fortified her heart. "I told you last night. This isn't the Wild, Wild West of Los Angeles. Crime isn't a problem."

"How can you be sure?" His gaze pierced her, held her captive so she couldn't turn away from the intensity of those deep brown eyes. "Weirdos and crazies know no boundaries. You don't know who was out there last night. Or why."

With an effort, she wrenched herself away from his gaze and started down the meadow toward the tree line. "Then let's see what we can find out."

She couldn't deny the glow of satisfaction his interest gave her, but she could resist it. She didn't need a man to protect her. She was perfectly capable of taking care of herself and Emily. "As a matter of fact, I do have a gun. Grandpa's shotgun. And I know how to use it. Granny taught me."

Dark memories inundated her. Five years ago, Granny had threatened to take that same shotgun down to Pinehurst to force Grady to marry Becca, but she'd talked her grandmother out of such drastic action. Much as Becca had thought she loved

Grady at the time, she'd had her pride, and she wouldn't marry any man who didn't want her, especially under duress.

"Maybe you should start locking your doors," Matt suggested. "At least until you figure out who's been prowling these woods and why."

Becca found the path that entered the woods and stepped into the shade of the trees. She knew these woods as well as her own house. She'd played here as a child, retreated here as a teenager and brought Emily here to teach her about her heritage. Becca felt comfortably at home in the dappled shade of the tall trees.

The path was narrow, so Matt followed behind her. "If no one uses these woods, how come there's a path?" he asked.

"There's more than one," Becca explained. "This is the path we use to harvest firewood. Others have been worn by hunters, children playing, even by dogs, deer and bear."

She heard Matt scuffing his foot at the hard-packed clay.

"Hard to make out tracks on this terrain," he observed.

"It rained yesterday," she reminded him. "If our midnight visitors left the path, we might find some traces."

Keeping her eyes on the ground for signs of anything unusual, she plunged deeper into the woods, glancing left and right among the understory of dogwoods and wild azaleas for anything out of the ordinary. Once they neared the spot where Matt had seen lights, she didn't have to search farther.

"Look at that." Becca pointed to a large patch of disturbed ground a few feet left of the path.

Matt followed her directions, stepped off the path and prodded the ground with the toe of his shoe. "Somebody's been digging here. Recently."

A shiver traveled down Becca's spine. "Question is, were they digging something up? Or burying it?"

CHAPTER SIX

Matt knelt in the damp leaves and plunged his hands into the loose soil. The disrupted area of dirt was only a few feet in diameter, and as he dug into the turned earth, he discovered that the excavation had been relatively shallow, less than a foot.

"It's not deep," he said. "And no sign of anything buried."

Becca knelt beside him, the fruity fragrance of her shampoo an intoxicating contrast to the musty scent of decaying leaves. "So we don't know if they dug up something to take away, or I startled them before they could bury what they intended."

Matt stood, dusted as much of the moist earth as he could from his hands and glanced around. "See any tracks?"

Becca rose to her feet and walked down the trail. "Here. Looks like a tennis-shoe print."

Matt joined her and placed his foot beside

the imprint in the damp soil. "Has to be a man's. It's larger than my foot, and I wear a twelve." He couldn't resist teasing her. "Don't suppose your Tarheel ghosts wear tennis shoes?"

Becca ignored his teasing and continued to survey the area. "There're more prints. Must have been at least two people."

"Where does this path lead?"

"It circles back to the main road. Comes out between our farm and the Ledbetters', where we passed the apple orchard on our way into town."

Matt tried to picture the local geography. "So your midnight visitors could have parked by the road, entered the woods from there, then returned to their car without anyone spotting them."

"Or hearing them," Becca said. "Our farms are several miles apart."

They searched the trail for several hundred feet, but found no more tracks or signs of digging.

"I'm going back to the house," Becca said, "in case Emily's awake. Want to look for more clues, Sherlock?"

"I prefer Spenser."

"Who?"

"Robert B. Parker's private detective. He's my favorite." Matt thought longingly of two

Parker novels sitting on the bookshelf in his Malibu house. He'd bought them to take on his South Pacific cruise. Now he wished he'd thought to pack them when Dwight had sent him here. Without television or any other nightlife, a good book seemed like his only hope for entertainment. "But at this point, Spenser would probably opt for coffee and doughnuts."

"Coffee we've got. But you'll have to settle for buttermilk biscuits."

"Suits me. Must be the mountain air. I'm hungry enough to eat anything." He hurried to catch up with Becca, who had already started up the path leading out of the woods.

"I wouldn't have taken you for a reader," she spoke over her shoulder.

"Why not?"

"Somehow I picture you always in a crowd. Hard to read with all that racket."

She'd pegged him correctly, he realized with a start. Ever since he'd begun his practice, he had been surrounded by people. His staff, nurses, patients, other doctors. And when he hadn't been working, he'd plunged into the Hollywood social scene with a vengeance. Constant parties with wall-to-wall people, inane conversations and too-loud music.

No wonder he'd needed a vacation. And suffered from that vague, underlying dissatisfaction that had haunted him the past year. He'd seldom had a solitary moment to himself.

He caught up with her as they left the woods, and walked beside her through the meadow. "You like to read?"

"Sure, but we're a long way from a library or bookstores."

"Ever thought of moving?"

The look she gave him couldn't have been more incredulous if he'd asked if she'd ever thought of cutting off her head. "Never."

"But you're so isolated here."

He could almost see the hackles rise on her neck. "Isolated from what? I have family, friends, neighbors. What more could I want?"

"Libraries, for a start," he said. "Theaters, shops —"

"Don't know how I've survived this long so far from Rodeo Drive," she said with a dramatic and definitely sarcastic sigh.

"Also restaurants, concerts and art galleries," he added.

Her smile was cynical. "Not to mention crime, traffic, pollution and all the other amenities of the rat race. I'll stay put on Warwick Mountain, thanks."

"Don't you sometimes feel like you're living in a time warp?"

She stopped to face him, and green fire flashed in her eyes. "Do I like the slower pace of mountain life? You bet. Do I feel deprived? Never. The news I glean from radio, occasional TV broadcasts and the Sunday paper makes me grateful I have such a safe and peaceful place to raise my daughter, away from the pressures and insanity of so-called modern life. I tried it once, and —"

She bit off whatever she was about to say, but not before he glimpsed the heartache in her eyes.

"And I didn't like it," she finished lamely.

Sorry to have stirred up what appeared to be bad memories, he changed the subject. "About those tracks in the woods . . ."

She started toward the house again. "What about them?"

"Do you have a local police force, someone to report them to?"

She shook her head. "All we have is the county sheriff. His deputies patrol this half of the county, but they'd lock me up for crazy if I called in a complaint of nothing more than strange lights and unidentified tracks."

Matt glanced around at the encircling

mountains and was struck by the seclusion of the Warwick farm. Becca's nearest neighbors were the McClains, just around the bend from her house.

"Do you have 911 emergency service?" he asked.

She nodded. "Paramedics and firefighters man the rescue station halfway between here and town. If we need a deputy, the sheriff's office dispatches the nearest car."

Matt recalled the long drive up the mountain from town to the village. No way to open up an engine and speed around those dangerous curves without flying off the road. "So if you called for help, it could take a while."

Becca shrugged. "I told you, crime's not a problem."

"Maybe I should stay here with you and Emily until you find out who was digging in the woods and why." He couldn't shake the protective instincts he felt toward Becca, didn't know where they'd come from. Other than with his mother, he'd never experienced those feelings toward a woman before.

Come to think of it, he realized with a twist of irony, most of the women he'd known in California were certified man-eaters, more than able to take care of themselves. He'd always been more concerned about protecting himself from them. But Becca had that appealing mix of strength and vulnerability that made him want to fight dragons for her.

"Look, Matt, we've been through this before. Even if I believed that Emily and I were in danger — which I don't — I can't afford to have you stay here. The scandal could cost me my job."

His temper flared. "And unsavory characters with homicidal tendencies creeping through your woods could cost you your life."

"Good grief," she said with a laugh that deflated his anger. "You've been reading too many mysteries. There's never been a murder on Warwick Mountain."

He wanted to say there was always a first time, but he knew when he was beaten. He'd have to move out today, but that didn't mean he couldn't keep an eye out for Becca and Emily from the village. Any vehicle heading up the mountain road toward Becca's would have to pass by the feed store. It shouldn't take him long to learn to recognize the regulars and spot a stranger.

Becca paused on the gravel path. "Go on inside. I'll join you in a minute."

She headed toward the barn. Matt entered the kitchen to the aroma of freshly brewed coffee, went to the sink and scrubbed the dirt from his hands. As he finished, Becca stepped inside and plunked a huge and obviously heavy wooden box on the floor.

"Here's Grandpa's tool kit. You can take it with you when you go."

Matt suppressed a sigh. He recognized here's-your-hat-what's-your-hurry when he heard it. She hadn't repeated her offer of giving him a hand with the feed-store measurements. Maybe he'd overstepped the line by suggesting he remain at her house.

Whatever the reason she'd closed him out, she hadn't forgotten her Southern hospitality. With a bright but brittle smile, she served him the best and biggest breakfast he'd ever tasted, what he figured would be his last meal in Becca's house.

"So how's Dr. Wonderful settling in?" Aunt Delilah sat at Becca's kitchen table, idly twirling the ice in her glass of tea.

Becca glanced away from the window where she'd been watching Emily give a picnic for her dolls in the backyard. "Don't know. Haven't talked to him since he left three days ago."

Delilah's gray eyebrows shot up in twin

peaks. "You just abandoned him?"

"Why is Matt Tyler my responsibility?"

Her aunt had keyed in too closely on the guilt Becca felt from ignoring the doctor, especially when his coming here was doing the community a favor. But she didn't dare spend time with him. More than village gossip, what she feared most was her response to him, an excitement that she hadn't been able to control. Avoidance was her best hope. She'd suffered heartbreak once. She wasn't about to set herself up for it again.

"You invited him here," Delilah reminded her.

"I invited Dwight Peyseur."

"And Matt's filling in."

"For the benefit of the community. Nothing to do with me," Becca insisted.

"Then he might as well go home." Delilah set her glass on the table with a thud. "Folks are too leery of his womanizing ways to let him treat them."

"Womanizing ways?"

"Does *People* magazine lie?"

Becca squirmed in her chair. She'd sneaked that issue out of Bessie's shop yesterday and read the article from start to finish. Twice. The story provided nothing concrete, nothing that proved Matt was anything more than a party animal, but the

120

report included enough innuendo for even the least literal of readers to jump to some fairly steamy conclusions. Implications were clear that Dr. Wonderful had put in a lot of time with Hollywood's plethora of female pulchritude.

"If people — and especially their children — need medical care," Becca insisted hotly, "what difference does it make if the man's dated every actress in Hollywood?"

"You think he has?" Delilah's voice raised an octave in interest.

"I know no more about his sex life than you do," Becca said with irritation. "The point is, why cut off their noses to spite their faces? He's here to offer his services, and folks should take advantage of him, particularly the McClains and the Dickenses."

"Takes time for people to trust him. Especially with their children."

"But we don't have time." Frustration edged Becca's voice. "He'll be leaving in a month."

Delilah pursed her lips, cast a quick glance around the kitchen as if to assure herself that they were alone, then leaned across the table like a conspirator. "I need your help, Rebecca."

At the desperation in her aunt's voice, Becca tensed. "What's wrong?"

"It's Jake's sister, Lydia."

"Is her sciatica worse?"

"She's ruining our marriage." Delilah's eyes clouded with tears. "In over fifty years, Jake and I have rarely had a cross word, but we've snapped at each other like quarreling dogs ever since that woman arrived."

"I can't keep her here," Becca said. "As soon as Matt's finished his additions to the feed store, I'll be introducing him to the community, helping him with his rounds."

Delilah shook her head. "Jake wouldn't hear of Lydia's leaving our house. Not while her sciatica has her in such pain. But she's driving me crazy, expecting me not only to wait on her hand and foot but to keep her entertained. Today's the first break I've had since she arrived, and I wouldn't be out of the house now if Susie Ledbetter hadn't volunteered to sit with her."

"I can come up now and then to stay with Lydia if you need to get out more," Becca offered.

"No, that's not what I meant." Delilah swept the kitchen with another surreptitious glance. "You can help better another way."

"How?"

Delilah took a deep breath. "Sneak Dr. Wonderful into Lydia's room."

"Aunt Delilah, what are you thinking?"

Becca wondered if her aunt had slipped a cog.

"Get your mind out of the gutter, Becca," Delilah snapped. "I need the doctor's medical expertise, not his —"

Her aunt fumbled for words.

"His what?" Becca couldn't help enjoying her aunt's embarrassment.

"Not his amorous abilities," Delilah said with a grimace.

"Sorry." Becca bit back a laugh. "I guess I misunderstood."

"You sure did," Delilah said sharply.

Becca tried to keep a straight face. "So, Lydia would let Matt examine her back?"

"She hasn't heard the gossip or read the magazine."

"What if Susie Ledbetter tells Lydia while she's there today?"

"I made her promise not to. Told her Lydia couldn't take any excitement." Delilah reached across the table and grabbed her hand. "I'm desperate, Becca. I have to have Lydia cured and out of my house or Jake and I will continue to be at each other's throats. The woman has to be the world's worst patient, and she's driving me past my limits!"

Becca took pity on her aunt. "What did Lydia's doctor in Blairsville recommend?"

"A few days of bed rest, then mild exercise, but Lydia refuses to get out of bed. Says the pain's too intense."

"You think she's faking?"

Delilah shrugged. "Hard to tell. I believe she's really suffering, but she's also milking her ailment for all the sympathy she can get. She has Jake wrapped around her little finger, but he's not the one waiting on her hand and foot."

"And you want me to sneak Matt in to see her?"

Delilah nodded. "Jake's going to town day after tomorrow. He'll be gone most of the day. If you could arrange it then?"

Conflicting emotions warred inside Becca. Delilah had just presented her with a perfect excuse to call on Matt without seeming personally interested. But seeing him again so soon threatened to weaken the defenses she'd thrown up against him. She had hoped for a few more days to gather her senses. Much as she'd like, however, she couldn't avoid him forever. And she couldn't turn her back on her aunt's obvious distress.

"I'll take supper down to him this evening," she said, "and arrange a visit to Lydia."

"Thank God," Delilah said. "I'm at my wit's end."

"That doesn't mean he'll cure her," Becca warned. "He may be no more help than her own doctor. After all, plastic surgery, not backs, is his specialty."

Delilah nodded and sipped her tea. "I understand. By the way, you're in for a surprise at the feed store. Bobbie Jo at the Shop-N-Go said a big eighteen-wheeler from Lowe's Home Improvement Warehouse pulled up in front of the feed store early yesterday. Took hours to unload. Lumber, drywall, a refrigerator, you name it. And this morning, a van from a furniture store all the way from Hickory made a delivery. With all they unloaded, you'd think the man was settling in for life."

"If you're a millionaire, you don't have to do without your comforts," Becca said with a touch of irony, "even in a derelict feed store. He can afford to order anything he wants, hire any help he needs. I'm surprised he hasn't advertised for a chef."

She glanced at her aunt and could almost see the wheels turning in Delilah's mind. "You're not thinking of applying for a job as his cook?"

Delilah looked aghast. "Jake would skin me alive. No, I was thinking I'll take Emily home to have supper with us. You take Matt his meal, then report to me when you pick up Emily."

"In front of Jake?"

Delilah's eyes widened in alarm. "You can't mention the house call while Jake's around. He won't have Dr. Wonderful touching his precious sister." Then she grinned. "But he'll be as interested as me in the details of what's going on in the feed store."

Becca nodded. "I'll call Emily for you."

Consumed with reluctance and anticipation, she went to the door to summon her daughter.

No big deal taking dinner to Matt, she assured herself. She was a grown woman in charge of her own destiny. She could control her response to the handsome doctor.

Couldn't she?

CHAPTER SEVEN

By the time Becca parked in front of the feed store a couple hours later, she had convinced herself that her attraction to Matt Tyler was a mere passing fancy. Nothing special about the man, she assured herself. And the fact that he was too handsome, too wealthy, too self-confident and too soon returning to the other side of the country lessened his appeal even more.

Nothing she couldn't handle.

Taking a deep breath, she slid from the car and removed the basket packed with his supper. No problem. She'd hand him the food, arrange a house call for Delilah's sister-in-law and be on her way.

Becca climbed the stairs of the loading dock to the shriek of a circular saw, gnawing its way through wood, which emanated from inside the store. The double front doors stood open wide to the fresh breeze, and late-afternoon sun gleamed through the high windows, illuminating the interior.

The sight before her tempted her to turn on her heel and flee.

Dressed in cargo shorts, a T-shirt, work boots and a tool belt slung low on his hips, Matt worked in a broad swath of sunlight from one of the high windows. A thin sheen of sweat slicked his face and the well-developed muscles of his arms flexed as he leaned across a makeshift workbench, guiding his saw through a two-by-four.

The man had obviously wielded more than a scalpel to acquire biceps like that, Becca thought. Of course, she reminded herself wryly, with his money, he probably had his own in-house gym and personal trainer. No wonder he looked like an action-movie star, unlike the scrawny, weathered and worn men of Warwick Mountain whose muscles had formed from the backbreaking labor needed to put food on their families' tables.

She held to that contrast as a shield against him, but she couldn't tear her glance away.

The saw ripped through the lumber, the noise stopped, and Matt looked up.

His smile when he caught sight of her drew her like a magnet, and she struggled to resist his charm.

"Hi." He set aside the saw, reached for a towel and wiped his face, chest and arms. "If I'd known you were coming, I'd have cleaned up."

"I don't want to interrupt your work," she said hurriedly and held up the basket. "I just stopped by to bring you supper."

He took an appreciative whiff of the air. "Smells wonderful. I've been eating frozen dinners for three days." He nodded toward the rear of the building. "We can eat in the other room."

"Oh, I can't stay —"

"But I want to show you what I've done."

Becca hesitated. She still had to arrange for Lydia's house call. "Well, maybe a minute."

"I've eaten alone the last three days. A friendly face across the table would be a treat." He pointed to the basket. "And if that thing's as full as it looks, there should be plenty for both of us." He glanced past her. "Where's Emily?"

"Having supper with Aunt Delilah," Becca said automatically, then bemoaned her lack of guile. She could have used her daughter as an excuse to escape quickly. As she glimpsed the alterations to the building's interior, however, her curiosity overcame her desire to retreat from Dr. Wonderful's tempting presence.

"You've accomplished a lot in a few days," she observed with genuine admiration.

"Here, let me take that and I'll show you around." Matt set her basket on the work-table, then waved an arm toward the half-formed wall. "I'm framing the front room now, the one I'll use to receive patients."

Becca bit her tongue. With all his hard work, she didn't have the heart to tell Matt that she doubted anyone would be using his services. Except Lydia, she reminded herself. And the McClains and the Dickenses, if she could persuade them.

"This way," he said. "I'll show you the rest."

Becca was no expert, but even to her untrained eye, the framing in the building appeared sturdy, straight and true. Professional. She had the impression that anything Matt set his hand to, he'd do well. He pulled back plastic sheeting that covered a door frame, and she stepped into the back room and stopped short in surprise.

"Needs paint on the drywall and a door," Matt said, "but this is where I live."

Matt had worked a minor miracle. Becca moved to the center of the room and circled slowly, taking in the details.

A trestle table in light wood flanked by

two matching chairs sat beneath a high window. Nearby stood a gleaming stainless-steel refrigerator, and a rolling wooden cart held a microwave oven and coffeemaker. Grouped atop a large geometric-print carpet in earth tones in the middle of the room were a cordovan leather sofa, two chairs and an entertainment center. On end tables flanking the sofa and chairs, bronze lamps with Arts and Crafts shades cast a soft ambient light throughout the area. In the corner by the bathroom sat an armoire that matched the entertainment center.

"How did you accomplish so much so fast?" she asked.

"I learned to do without sleep when I was an intern," he explained. "Working late, it didn't take long to frame and drywall. And less than an hour to arrange the furniture."

A tall, narrow packing box leaned against the wall next to the armoire. "What's that?" she asked.

"A shower unit. There's just enough room to squeeze it next to the toilet, but I wanted your okay before I installed it."

"That's fine," Becca stammered, still trying to comprehend how much the man had completed in so little time. Not only the work, but also the amount of thought and planning that had gone into the project.

Matt had needed more than money alone to turn this corner of an abandoned building into an attractive, livable space. Although, judging from the obvious quality, he hadn't skimped on cost.

"Where do you sleep?" she asked.

"Sofa makes into a bed. Not that I've used it much yet. Sit down. Try it out."

Again Becca hesitated. If she was going to ask a favor for Lydia, however, she had to be polite. She perched on the edge of the sofa. The smooth, glove-soft leather caressed the back of her bare legs and the plump cushions seemed to embrace her.

Matt went to the refrigerator, removed a bottle of wine and took two glasses from the shelf beneath the microwave. "I've been waiting for someone to help me celebrate."

"Celebrate?"

"That I haven't lost my touch as a carpenter. Guess it's like riding a bicycle. It all came back quickly once I started working." He uncorked the bottle with distinct expertise, filled two glasses and handed Becca one.

She eyed the drink warily. She hadn't drunk wine since her days in Pinehurst. Alcohol clouded her thoughts, loosened her inhibitions and made her maudlin. She needed a clear head to deal with Matt.

"A toast?" he asked.

Thinking quickly, Becca clinked her glass to his. "To better medical care for the folks of Warwick Mountain."

"A noble sentiment," Matt said, "and one I endorse, but this isn't the Rotary Club." He touched his glass to hers. "To friendship."

He drank his wine, but she didn't touch hers. She wanted to be his friend. Wanted it too much. Her relationship with Grady had begun with friendship.

And ended in disaster.

"Something wrong?" he asked.

"No." She tossed him a false smile and chugged her wine to cover her discomfort. The smooth, cool liquid slid down her throat with ease, and she drank again. "But if you want your fried chicken while it's still warm, you'd better eat now."

He retrieved the basket from the front room, set it on the table and began removing its contents. "Oh, man, fried chicken, potato salad, homemade pickles, biscuits and peach cobbler. Becca, you've saved my life."

The wine hit her stomach and spread a rosy glow throughout her body. "Hope you enjoy it. I have to go."

She set down her glass and headed for the

doorway, but he caught her hand. "Please, stay and eat with me."

"I can't. I only came to —" She clamped her lips shut. Her head buzzed from the wine. Why not, she thought. Truth was truth. "I only came to ask a favor."

"Granted," he said, "but only if you'll stay for dinner."

She'd walked straight into his trap. "You don't know what the favor is."

He pulled out a chair for her at one end of the table, then topped off her wineglass and placed it in front of her. "Don't have to know. I know you. You wouldn't ask me to do anything immoral or illegal."

"Or impossible?" Without thinking, she sipped the wine.

"That might take a little longer." His grin was infectious as he tugged his chair next to hers and began filling two plates from the dishes she'd brought.

"Any more midnight visitors, strange lights?" He spooned enough potato salad onto her plate for three people.

She shrugged. "Haven't been awake to check. And Emily hasn't noticed anyone, either."

"Have you looked in the woods to see if someone's been digging again?" He handed her the plate.

"Should I?" The thought hadn't occurred to her. Was she being insensitive to possible danger, or had her introduction to Matt addled her brains?

His expression was solemn, accentuating the handsome contours of his face. "Wouldn't hurt — if you don't go into the woods alone."

She couldn't help laughing. The woods were like an extension of her home and she felt as safe there as she did in her own living room. "I'm too old to believe in the bogeyman."

He scowled. "Don't be. There're some real monsters out there. They pop up on television and in the newspaper every day."

She didn't know whether to feel flattered by his concern or annoyed at his implication she couldn't take care of herself. No one had really worried about her since Granny died, and she decided she liked having someone care about her welfare.

He dug into his potato salad with gusto, his hunger apparently unimpeded by thoughts of criminals. But his next question took away her appetite.

"You are locking your doors now?" he asked.

She felt her cheeks flush with guilt. "I did the first night. . . ."

"And since?"

"I forgot."

He used what Granny would have called "colorful language" before she'd have washed his mouth out with soap. "Don't you care what happens to you? Or at least to Emily?"

"Of course." She shot her answer back at him. "But you're asking me to change a habit of a lifetime."

"I could call you every night and remind you."

"Why would you do that?"

"Because I care what happens to you." His intense brown eyes glowed with an emotion she couldn't name, didn't want to.

"You don't have a phone," she said, breathless and not knowing why.

"It's being installed tomorrow. Patients will need a way to contact me."

In a pig's eye, she thought, recalling the censure he faced, but she'd allow him to finish his meal before she broached that unpleasant fact.

He set down his fork, his former expression replaced by a look of obvious self-satisfaction. "I know the perfect solution."

"To what?" Had he read her thoughts about the community's collective cold shoulder?

"Your security problem."

"I didn't realize I had one," she admitted dryly.

"You need a dog." His voice was triumphant, as if he'd just found the answer to world peace. Being pleased with himself gave him a boyish appearance she found entirely too engaging.

She swallowed her bite of chicken. "I can't afford a dog."

He shook his head. "You can get one at the pound. Free."

She adored dogs, but his idea wasn't practical. "A watchdog? An animal that size would eat me out of house and home."

"You don't need a big dog. A little terrier makes a lot of noise. It could sound the alarm, scare off intruders."

His enthusiasm was contagious, and the suggestion wasn't entirely without merit. "Emily's been pestering me for a dog."

"Where's the nearest animal shelter?"

"In town."

"Let me take you and Emily in tomorrow. You can pick out a pet."

"Whoa, not so fast. Life may be more spontaneous where you come from. Here, we like to think things over for a while before taking action."

She couldn't help feeling gratified by his

interest. She and Emily had been on their own too long, with only Aunt Delilah to take an interest in their well-being.

"Didn't mean to pressure you," he said. "But I'll be happy to drive you to the pound if you decide you want a dog."

"Do you have a dog?"

"I'm a sucker for dogs." A wistful expression flitted across his face. "Couldn't afford one growing up. Didn't have time for one in medical school."

"And now?"

"I'm hardly ever home. Wouldn't be fair to have an animal under those circumstances."

"If you had time for a dog, what kind would you choose?"

"A full house. A golden retriever, a black Lab, one of those fluffy little bichon frises that look like a powder puff, and a Chihuahua. For starters."

His eyes held a yearning that embarrassed her and made her look away. Another soft spot in the supposedly hard, cyncial shell of Dr. Wonderful. The man loved dogs. He was becoming harder to resist by the second.

To return to less treacherous ground, she changed the subject. "Aren't you curious about the favor you promised me for having supper with you?"

"I figured you'd get around to asking eventually."

She explained about Jake's sister, Lydia, and the havoc her sciatica was wreaking on Delilah's marriage.

"I'll be glad to take a look at her," he said. "After all, that's why I'm here."

Becca shifted uneasily in her chair. "It's not that simple."

"Maybe not, but there're some new treatments —"

"I'm not talking about the sciatica." Her voice came out sharper than she intended. She gulped more of her wine to calm her nerves.

Matt set down the chicken leg he'd been eating, wiped his hands on his napkin and laid it beside his plate. "What are you talking about?"

She shook her head, not knowing how to begin. "It sounds so silly when I say it out loud."

He cocked an eyebrow, looking for an instant like a mischievous little boy instead of one of Hollywood's handsomest men. "Want to whisper it instead?"

She laughed, then turned somber again. "I have to sneak you into the house at Aunt Delilah's while Uncle Jake's gone to town day after tomorrow."

Matt groaned and slumped in his chair. "Don't tell me. It's the Dr. Wonderful curse, isn't it?"

Becca finished her second glass of wine and nodded. "People see you as exotic, dangerous. Fascinating to talk about, interesting to meet, but they don't want you treating them. I know it sounds crazy, but that's the way mountain folk are."

"Crazy?" His impish look returned.

"Slow to trust, especially when they think of you as if you came from another planet."

"Don't remind me. Planet Hollywood." He shoved his fingers through his hair in obvious frustration. "Sometimes I feel like I've landed on an alien world."

She rose to her feet, surprised to find the room tilting ever so slightly. She set aside the plates, and dished up cobbler. Very carefully. She'd definitely had too much wine, and in spite of the food, it had gone straight to her head.

"How come Delilah's willing for me treat her sister-in-law?" Matt asked before digging into his dessert.

"Desperation." Becca sank into her chair, happy to stop the room from spinning.

"And why has Lydia agreed? Her pain's that bad?"

"They've held her incommunicado."

"She doesn't know about Dr. Wonderful?"

"Apparently she's the only person on the mountain who doesn't."

As if the full implication of the situation had just struck him, Matt set down his spoon, and emotion sparked in his eyes. Whether anger or frustration, Becca couldn't tell.

"You mean *no one* wants me to treat them?" he asked.

"I'm sorry."

He shoved back from the table, stood and glared at her. "Then what am I doing here?"

Chapter Eight

"Lizzie McClain," Becca said, summing up in one word the most important reason Matt had come to Warwick Mountain.

The anger that had stiffened Matt's spine seemed to drain out of him, and he sank back in his seat. "You think there's a chance her parents will relent?"

"I'm counting on it. I'll do everything I can to talk them into Lizzie's surgery."

"At least you'll have some improvements on your clinic." His voice and expression reflected more than a touch of irony.

"Fixing this place up was your idea," she reminded him, then quickly added, "but I am grateful."

He sighed. "If I'd known I'd be this useless, I'd have taken that South Pacific cruise."

"You gave up your vacation to come here?" He'd sacrificed his time off. Sacrificed it for nothing if she couldn't break down the walls of prejudice that faced him. Guilt gnawed at her.

"Dwight and I close the practice for several weeks every summer. Makes getting away easier without putting a burden on each other."

Becca shook her head and was horrified to find tears springing to her eyes. Had to be the wine. She'd never been a weepy kind of woman. "I'm sorry."

He leaned toward her, his eyes bright with sympathy, and closed his hand over hers. Her senses leaped at the warmth of his skin against hers — until her brain kicked in, and she jerked her hand away.

"Hey," he said with a surprising gentleness that made her want to throw herself into his arms. "It's not your fault. You're the one who's trying to help."

To her added horror, the unwanted tears spilled over and splashed down her cheeks. "But I didn't know Dr. Dwight would break his wrist. Or that he'd send Dr. Wonderful in his place. Or that everyone would be so blasted suspicious of you." She swiped the traitorous tears from her cheeks with the backs of her hands. "Nothing's gone the way I've planned."

He stood again, grasped her by the elbows and practically lifted her from her chair.

With a gentle tug, he led her toward the sofa, sat in the corner and pulled her down into the crook of his arm.

"You're too hard on yourself," he said softly. "You don't give yourself enough credit for all you do for these people. It isn't your fault they're too stubborn to take advantage of it."

Alarms sounded in her head, urging her to stand and run, but her heart encouraged her to snuggle deeper into the warm circle of his arm.

She couldn't think straight. Couldn't resist the unexpected comfort of his embrace, the obvious concern in his eyes. Talk about a bedside manner. Matt had it in spades.

Suddenly she realized exactly how much danger she'd placed herself in. She could resist handsome. She could resist fame. She could even resist wealth. But what defenses did she have against a man so innately *nice*? So transparently kind?

She rose on wobbly legs, intending to leave, but only made it as far as the opposite end of the sofa before common sense demanded she sit again. She was in no condition to drive, especially on mountain roads.

"Maybe I'd better have a cup of coffee," she suggested.

He cocked an eyebrow. "Tipsy?"

She nodded, feeling sheepish. "I must have drunk more wine than I realized."

He filled her coffee cup and brought it to her. "Females metabolize alcohol more quickly and efficiently than males. Add to that your slighter weight, and even two glasses of wine can pack a punch."

"They teach you that at medical school?" She chugged her coffee, hoping to banish the wine's effect.

"Yep, that and the fact that consuming caffeine after too much alcohol only produces a wide-awake drunk." His wide grin enhanced his appeal, and she glanced away.

"I'm not drunk."

"Glad to hear it. Wouldn't want to be accused of debauching the local schoolmarm."

"Been there, done that," she replied, then horrified by her admission, sat upright so quickly she spilled her coffee.

"No problem. I'll get it." Matt grabbed a napkin and sopped the liquid from the leather sofa, then turned his calm gaze on her. "Want to talk about it?"

Neither his voice nor his expression held censure or prurient interest, but Becca's face flamed with embarrassment nonetheless. "Why would I want to talk about the most humiliating time in my life?"

"To prove it doesn't hold any power over you?" He settled next to her on the sofa, but without invading her space.

"Don't tell me," she said with a nervous laugh. "You also interned in psychiatry."

His deep, rich laugh echoed through the open rafters of the old building. "No, but a doctor sees people when they're most vulnerable. I've learned from experience that encouraging patients to talk about what's bothering them helps them deal with it."

"I'm not your patient." Her voice held an edge sharper than she'd intended.

Matt, however, didn't blink. "No, but I'd like you to be my friend. From what you've told me, I'm guessing you're probably the only friend I'll have here."

She felt instantly contrite. He was only trying to be helpful, and she'd gone on the offensive. "Sorry I snapped at you."

"Don't apologize. I was sticking my nose where it doesn't belong and deserved to have it slapped."

She arched her neck and leaned her head against the back of the sofa, still feeling the wine working its way through her blood-stream, suffusing her with a delicious peace-fulness. She was enjoying Matt's company. Too much. She couldn't remember ever feeling so relaxed, so at ease with a man.

Not even Grady.

"You've been hurt, haven't you?" he asked gently.

"Hasn't everyone?"

"Emily's father?"

She raised her head and met his kind, accepting gaze. "How did you know?"

"Doesn't take a Sherlock Holmes — or Spenser — to draw that conclusion. Especially since Emily doesn't seem to know anything about her own dad."

Becca struggled to escape the soft, enveloping depths of the sofa. "I'd better go."

"Don't leave. Not unless you'll let me drive you home."

"Then how would you get back?"

"I'd walk."

"It's three miles!"

He grinned. "But it's all downhill. On the other hand, you can stay until your head clears."

"So you can grill me with more personal questions?" She tried for an indignant tone, but couldn't summon the outrage. In spite of his probing queries, Matt's attitude had been nothing but sympathetic.

"No more questions," he said. "I promise."

She sank back into the cushions, consumed by the sudden desire to share the story she'd never told anyone but Granny. She'd been too humiliated, devastated, embarrassed. Now, over five years later, those events still had the same hold on her. Maybe Matt was right, and confession was good for the soul. If telling Dr. Wonderful about Grady would purge the jerk from her memories, sharing her disgrace would be worth it.

"Emily's father lives in Pinehurst," she began. "That's in the eastern part of the state."

"You don't have to do this," Matt said. "We can talk about the weather. Apparently it's always changing here in the mountains."

Becca shook her head. "I should talk about him. You're right about the power he has over me. I've let it fester like an untreated wound."

He nodded. "Go ahead. Where wounds are concerned, the doctor is in."

His compassion amazed her. She'd underestimated him, thinking him as superficial as the magazine article had painted him. She was discovering a depth to Matt Tyler she hadn't expected.

"Know why I became a teacher?" she asked.

"So you could have the *big* desk?"

His joking pleased her, made the telling

easier. "My parents died in a car accident when I was younger than Emily, and Granny brought me to live with her. Until I went away to college at Chapel Hill, I rarely left the mountain, except for attending high school in town and making an occasional visit to Asheville."

"The big city?"

"Biggest one I knew. But that's my point. Education opened up the world for me. It didn't matter that I hadn't traveled the States, visited foreign countries or been to the moon. I experienced all those things. And more. Learning was the most exciting thing that ever happened to me, and I wanted to become a teacher to share that excitement with others."

"I had a few teachers who felt like that," Matt said. "They always inspired me."

"Only a few?"

"Ever heard the expression that truth is the first casualty of war?"

Becca nodded.

"In South L.A., idealism was the first casualty of teaching. But I'm interrupting. Please, go on with your story."

She tried to picture the cool and polished man before her in the rough-and-tumble neighborhood he referred to — and failed. Wealth and privilege seemed so ingrained in the man, it was impossible to imagine him without them.

She returned to her story. "With Granny's help and a scholarship, I was able to go to college. Got my teaching degree. Granny wanted me to come back to Warwick Mountain, but I'd had a taste of the outside world at Chapel Hill, and I wasn't ready to come home."

"You stayed in the state. Why didn't you go somewhere more exotic, like Alaska or New York City?"

"Much as I wanted new experiences, I realized Granny was getting older and having health problems. I didn't want to be so far away, I couldn't reach her within a few hours of driving."

"Why Pinehurst?"

"It's a resort town — the closest I could find to exotic near to home. People come from all over to play the golf courses there. I figured if I couldn't travel, I could at least meet interesting people from different parts of the world."

"Makes sense." He got up, grabbed the coffeepot, topped off her cup and filled one for himself before sitting again.

She drank more coffee and, in spite of Matt's claim to the contrary, could feel the effects of the wine gradually dissipating.

"When the opening for a third-grade teacher in Pinehurst was posted at the job fair the month before I graduated, I applied and was accepted immediately."

"Sounds like an auspicious beginning," he said with a hint of admiration in his voice. "You must have had quite a résumé."

"Thanks for the compliment, but I think the teacher shortage had the greater impact on my speedy hiring."

"So you moved to Pinehurst?"

"Only after spending most of the summer with Granny. We drove down together to find me an apartment and for her to see my school. I was restless to move and begin my new life, but Granny wasn't well, so I stayed in Warwick Mountain as long as I could. I'd have been better off if I'd never left." She couldn't keep the bitterness from her voice.

"But you wouldn't have Emily," Matt noted. "She's a remarkable little girl."

"You're right." She felt the resentment ease its hold on her. "Having Emily is worth all that happened."

The sun had set, the air had cooled, and Becca, dressed in shorts and a sleeveless blouse, shivered.

"I need a fireplace," Matt said, observing her shivers. "Or at least a baseboard heater." He walked to the armoire, pulled out the bulky fisherman's sweater he'd worn the morning he met the Habersham sisters and handed it to her. "But this will have to do."

"Thanks." Becca slid the garment over her head, and its volume engulfed her all the way to her thighs. She pushed back the drooping sleeves to expose her hands, and snuggled comfortably into its soft warmth that made her feel as if she had slipped into his arms. The image wrecked her concentration. "Where was I?"

"You'd just moved to Pinehurst." He pulled on a forest-green sweater that accentuated the golden sun streaks in his hair and returned to his seat.

Maybe the dropping temperature, along with the coffee, had cleared her head, because she no longer felt the dizzying effects from the wine. "It's an old story, one I'm sure you've heard a thousand times —"

"I never heard *your* story," he said, "but if telling it's too painful —"

Becca waited for the sharp stab of hurt that usually surfaced whenever she thought of Grady, but it didn't appear. "I don't want to bore you."

"Rebecca Warwick." His remarkable eyes bored into hers. "You're the least boring woman I ever met."

She laughed with surprise. "I find that

hard to believe."

He scowled. "You calling me a liar?"

"Considering the women you've been rumored to hang out with, I'd say you're more like a shameless flatterer."

His frown remained. "Why would I do that?"

She shrugged. "I learned the hard way I'm not very good at judging men's motives."

The chiseled lines of his face dissolved into an expression of concern so intense she had to look away. "Your hurt runs deep, doesn't it?"

She lifted her chin, glad she could say honestly, "Not as deep as I once thought. I guess time does heal all wounds."

"And wounds all heels?" he added with a smile.

"One can only hope." She returned his smile, then sobered again. "My first year of teaching was a mixture of ecstasy and terror."

"Terror?"

"As much as they taught me in college, I wasn't prepared for the day-to-day challenges and unexpected crises of the classroom. I've discovered since, after talking with more experienced teachers, that you have to dive in over your head and learn as you go."

"Sounds a lot like practicing medicine," he observed.

She folded her legs beneath her and pulled his sweater over her knees to warm them. She felt as comfortable with him as if she were sitting in her own living room, talking with Granny.

"In January of my first teaching year," she continued, "the chamber of commerce held a teacher-appreciation breakfast at a local resort owned by Raymond Sadler. All the teachers were invited. We sat at tables with the local businesspeople, and I ended up next to Grady Sadler, son of the resort's owner."

"Love at first sight?" Matt asked gently.

Becca grimaced. "I thought so at the time. I was too green and inexperienced to know better. Grady was handsome, wealthy and charming." *All the qualities you possess,* she thought. "And most mesmerizing of all, he seemed totally interested in me." She threw Matt a self-effacing grin. "I didn't have a chance."

"How old were you?"

"Barely twenty-one, but I'd led a sheltered life on Warwick Mountain. In many ways, even after four years of college, I was totally naive." She snuggled deeper into the corner of the sofa. "Unlike, I'm sure, the women you meet in Hollywood."

"They may arrive naive," Matt admitted, "but the social scene is a jungle. Hard to remain innocent among all that self-serving hedonism."

"What about your own innocence?" she challenged, amazed by her boldness.

"Lost that when my mother died." The pain in his expression spoke volumes. "I knew then the world was a cruel and dangerous place." He shook his head and the hurt in his eyes cleared. "But that's my story. I want to hear the rest of yours."

"There's not much else to tell. Grady sent me flowers. Took me to all the best restaurants. Invited himself up to my apartment. You can guess the rest. I was so bowled over by the attentiveness of Pinehurst's most eligible bachelor, I forgot everything Granny had ever taught me. By spring break, I realized I was pregnant."

"What did Grady think of that?" Matt asked.

"He was horrified. And horrid. Asked me if I was sure the baby was his."

"Ouch," Matt said with sympathy.

"His callous attitude destroyed the fantasy I'd created around him. Oh, he was handsome, wealthy and charming all right, but about as shallow as a saucer, and interested only in himself."

"So he wouldn't marry you?"

"He said he would, but he kept delaying setting a date."

"You would have married a man you didn't love?" Matt shot her a disbelieving look.

"He was the father of my unborn baby, and I believe every child needs a father." As she spoke the words, she realized that Grady's refusal to marry her had probably saved her from a living hell. And eventual divorce.

"One day," she continued, "a week before the school term ended, his father came to my apartment. He offered me a check for a hundred thousand dollars if I'd leave town and keep my baby's paternity a secret."

"Is that why Emily doesn't know who her father is?" Matt appeared shocked.

"We have a word in Warwick Mountain for women who take money for sex," Becca said hotly, "and I'm not one of those. I tore Mr. Sadler's check into tiny pieces and threw him out. As soon as school ended, I resigned my position and came home to have Emily."

"And you never heard from Grady?"

"Not directly. I read in the Asheville paper when he married the daughter of a state senator. I'm sure wherever he is now, his daddy's still buying his way out of trouble."

"You're lucky to be rid of him," Matt said forcefully.

Becca sighed. "I know. I just wish I could rid myself of feeling like a fool."

"Not a fool," Matt said with a shake of his head. "Just human."

She eyed him closely then, wondering if a woman had ever duped him as Grady had her, but she couldn't imagine it. Matt seemed too savvy, too in control.

"Was it rough coming back here?" he asked.

"Granny was wonderful. She saw how miserable I was and never let an I-told-you-so slip, even if she thought it."

"I was thinking more of the neighbors. They may be fine people, as you've insisted, but open-mindedness doesn't seem one of their more prevalent virtues." His voice held a strange note, and for the first time, she realized he'd apparently been more wounded than she'd realized by their ostracism.

"Oh, I caused a scandal, all right." She allowed herself a rueful smile. "If it had been up to me, I'd have hidden in Granny's house for the rest of my life and never shown my face. But Granny had other ideas."

"Must have been hard for you."

Becca nodded, remembering. "At first, but Granny was right. Better to face people and hold my head up than to act ashamed. When we went to church, people would ask when I was returning to Pinehurst to teach. 'She's not,' Granny would say. 'She's staying here to have her baby.' "

Granny had stood like a ramrod and faced them down, Becca recalled proudly. " 'Didn't know Becca was married,' the bolder ones would comment. Granny would look them in the eye and say in her calm but firm way, 'Becca's a single mother. She's going to need our help.' "

"I wish I could have met her," Matt said. "She sounds like quite a woman."

"She was. I really miss her. By the time Emily was born, thanks to Granny, most of the scandal — or at least any open sign of it — had died. So far, Emily's been lucky. No one's taunted her about not having a father."

A puzzled frown creased Matt's forehead. "If the local school board is so hung up on morality, how'd you convince them to hire you, considering the circumstances of Emily's birth?"

"When Emily was a year old, Miss Carlisle, who'd been teaching here forever, had a stroke. I filled in as a substitute. The board liked my work, and offered me a permanent position." She stifled the urge to yawn and glanced at her watch. "It's past Emily's bedtime. She's probably fallen asleep at Aunt Delilah's."

"Want me to drive you?" Matt offered again.

Becca stood and said, "No, thanks. I'm fine. Really. But I have to hurry."

She rushed through the building, out the door and down the stairs. Matt caught up with her when she reached her car. He grasped her shoulders and turned her toward him. "I haven't thanked you for bringing dinner."

"No need —"

He dipped his head and kissed her, stopping her from saying more. The pressure of his lips at first was gentle, and he tasted deliciously of coffee and a masculine essence. Wrapping his arms around her, he drew her close. The excitement of his kiss scrambled her brain, short-circuited her reasoning, and she lifted her arms, twined them around his neck, and felt the jolt of his kiss all the way to her toes.

What was she doing?

Before she could react and pull away, he released her. Cupping her face in his hands, he gazed into her eyes, his own shining with a fierce brilliance in the moonlight.

"Grady Sadler," he said through gritted teeth, "was an idiot."

Before Becca could reply, Matt turned on his heel and strode up the stairs to the loading dock. He stopped there and called back to her. "I'll pick you up day after tomorrow for our visit to Lydia. Maybe we can stop and see the McClains at the same time."

Becca nodded, too shaken by the effects of his kiss to speak.

"Call me," he said, "if you decide to get a dog. And don't forget to lock your doors tonight."

She nodded again. With legs trembling, she climbed into her car and drove away. In her rearview mirror, she could see Matt silhouetted by the light from the double doors, watching her leave.

She was halfway to Aunt Delilah's, still shaken by his unexpected kiss and her reaction, before she realized she still wore Matt's sweater.

CHAPTER NINE

Matt manhandled a sheet of drywall against the studs and held it in place with his shoulder while securing it with screws. He'd overslept this morning and was off to a late start, primarily because he hadn't been able to sleep the night before.

Becca had kept him awake.

Not that she'd been there. Her absence had been the problem. He kept reliving that kiss, and his mind hadn't been able to let her go.

Or his heart.

Never had a woman possessed him so totally as the wonderfully simple — or should he say simply wonderful — schoolteacher. He'd felt abandoned last night when she drove away, and his new living quarters, which had suited him to a T before, had suddenly seemed barren and lonely.

His brain felt fuzzy from lack of sleep, and

if he'd been home in Malibu, he'd have taken a long swim in the cold Pacific to clear his mind.

Of course, if he were at home in Malibu, he wouldn't have met the schoolmarm and he wouldn't be having this problem.

The mountain air was affecting his reasoning. Why should Becca Warwick, beautiful as she was, he argued with himself, have a hold on him that none of Hollywood's most glamorous women had managed?

Was it because he was lonely, a fish out of water in this isolated mountain village and she was a very attractive, friendly face?

That argument wouldn't wash. She was polite, hospitable and appreciative of his willingness to treat patients in the village, but friendly? She obviously disapproved of him and his lifestyle. And he'd had to twist her arm to convince her to stay for dinner last night.

Then why had she opened up to him and shared the story of the most humiliating time of her life?

That answer was easy. The wine had gone to her head. Becca apparently wasn't used to drinking. That fact gave him pause. He'd dated petite actresses who could imbibe all night, and still be bright-eyed and pert hours later.

Even though he was a doctor, for the first time he felt suddenly offended that these women had abused their bodies so flagrantly.

Matt stopped, holding a sheet of drywall in midair. He'd never thought that way before about the women he'd dated. Drug and alcohol abuse were the norm for the Hollywood social scene. That explained why meeting a woman like Becca was like a breath of fresh air.

Was he falling for a Goody Two-shoes?

Not a Goody Two-shoes, he realized with a jolt, but a woman who had self-respect.

So much self-respect that the first guy she'd dated got her pregnant?

Matt shook his head. So much self-respect that she tore up a hundred-thousand-dollar check, a bribe for her silence and a fortune for a woman like Becca, rather than let herself be bought off by a worthless scum and his father.

That self-respect was one of the main differences between Becca and the other women Matt had known. The others would have sold their souls for the right part, the trendiest look, the best connections. Becca's values were as deeply rooted as Warwick Mountain itself.

So why should he expect a woman like

her to have anything to do with Dr. Wonderful, stud to the stars?

Matt clenched his teeth in anger. He wasn't the man the magazine had portrayed. Too close for comfort maybe, but he wasn't as degenerate as the unrealistic picture the article had painted. Sure, he'd partied too hard, spent too much, passed his spare time in frivolous pursuits and enjoyed his freedom, but he'd never broken a woman's heart. He'd never made promises he wouldn't keep. Certainly never left a woman high, dry and pregnant like that slimeball Grady.

Was he trying to convince himself that he was worthy of a woman like Becca?

Matt wasn't talking about *marrying* her. He just wanted to be her friend.

But he had been thinking of marriage —

A high-pitched squeaky voice behind him jolted Matt from his churning thoughts. "Whatcha doing, mister?"

Matt fumbled the drywall sheet back onto the sawhorses and turned toward the door. A small, slight figure, a child dressed in shorts, a T-shirt and well-worn sneakers with a Braves baseball cap pulled low on his face stood in the shadows.

"I'm hanging drywall," Matt said.

"Why?"

"To make an office."

"What kind of office?"

"A doctor's office." Although Matt wondered why he bothered, after what Becca had told him last night.

"Where's the doctor?" the boy, who appeared to be around eight years old, asked.

"You're looking at him."

"Didn't know doctors did work."

"Some doctors have been known to break a sweat," Matt said dryly.

"Are you the doctor who's going to fix my face?"

Now the boy had Matt's complete attention. "What's wrong with your face?"

The boy stepped forward into the glare from the electrical lights Matt had suspended to illuminate his work area. He immediately noted the scarred and puckered skin of the boy's right arm exposed by his short-sleeved T-shirt. The boy whipped off his ball cap, revealing a thick thatch of red hair that stood in unruly clumps where it hadn't been matted by the cap's band. Bright blue eyes confronted Matt, as if daring him to flinch at the boy's appearance. Only Matt's years of training allowed him to gaze dispassionately at the boy's scars, which marred the right side of his face as completely as a wealth of freckles covered the left.

"Are you Jimmy Dickens?"

"Yeah. How'd you know?"

"Miss Warwick told me about you."

At the mention of his teacher, the boy's face softened into an expression of unmistakable puppy love. With a start, Matt realized he knew just how the kid felt.

Shaking off his feelings for Becca, Matt glanced behind the boy toward the door. "Are your parents with you?"

"Ma's up at the church, meeting with the ladies' society."

"Does she know you're here?" Matt asked.

Jimmy looked guilty. "She said I could buy gum at the Shop-N-Go."

"How long is her meeting?" Matt asked.

"Till lunchtime."

"I was about to have coffee. You want some milk and cookies? Then you can tell me what happened to your face."

Jimmy hesitated, as if well aware he was violating his mother's instructions.

"Tell you what," Matt suggested. "I'll bring them out to the loading dock, so you can watch for your mom, in case she gets out of her meeting early. That okay with you?"

Jimmy nodded, and Matt went into the

back room. He filled a mug with coffee, loaded chocolate chip cookies from their package onto a plate and added a glass of milk. When he carried the snacks out front, Jimmy was sitting on the edge of the dock, swinging his legs over the side. Matt handed the boy the plate and sat beside him.

"So," Matt said as casually as possible. "What happened to your face?"

Jimmy swigged his milk, leaving a white mustache above his upper lip. "Ma burned me."

"How'd that happen?"

"It was an accident. Ma loves me. She wouldn't have done it on purpose."

"Of course not," Matt agreed.

"Sometimes she cries when she looks at me." Sadness etched the boy's face. "She feels so bad at what she done."

"Tell me about the accident."

"It was two years ago when I was just a little kid. Ma was fixing to fry green tomatoes." His sadness disappeared and his blue eyes brightened. "She makes the best fried green tomatoes in the county. Wins all the ribbons at the county fair."

Matt sipped his coffee and prayed for patience. Apparently Jimmy would have to meander through his tale at his own pace.

"Ma had the lard heating in the frying

pan, but the baby started crying. While she was checking on the baby, the lard caught fire. I hollered for Ma and asked her what to do. She came running, grabbed the burning pan with a pot holder and told me to open the back door." Jimmy took a bite of cookie and chewed thoughtfully, as if remembering. "We was all afraid the house would catch fire."

"But it didn't?"

Jimmy shook his head. "It was my fault."

"That the grease caught fire?"

"That Ma tripped. I shoulda stood behind the door, not in front of it. She stumbled over my foot and the burning grease sloshed all over me."

Matt's heart went out to the little boy. "That must have hurt."

Jimmy nodded solemnly and swallowed a mouthful of cookie. "It hurt something powerful. My clothes caught fire, and Ma rolled me in the grass. Then she took me inside and coated my burns with butter. Said that would soothe them, but it didn't."

Matt suppressed a scowl. Apparently knowledge of the uselessness — and potential harm — of that old wives' remedy hadn't yet reached into the back roads of Warwick Mountain.

"When I couldn't stop crying —" Jimmy

hung his head with an embarrassed expression "— Ma called the County Fire and Rescue, and they sent the paramedics."

"I would have cried, too," Matt assured him, "if I'd been burned like that. Takes strong painkillers to numb that kind of pain."

"The paramedics musta used them. They gave me a shot that knocked me out. Next thing I knew, I woke up in the hospital in town." His voice dropped to almost a whisper. "And it still hurt."

Matt cursed silently. He'd seen the tiny hospital in town when he'd gone to buy supplies. Better than a walk-in clinic, but definitely not equipped to handle an emergency such as Jimmy's.

Life sure wasn't fair. If Jimmy had been living in Los Angeles or some other major city when he'd been burned, he'd have been instantly airlifted by helicopter to the nearest burn-trauma unit, where he would have received immediate specialized care. That treatment would not only have reduced his suffering, it would have lessened the amount of excessive scarring.

"Did they move you to a special burn unit?" Matt asked.

"A few days later."

The boy's answer confirmed Matt's suspicions about the extent of his scarring.

"Guess you spent a lot of time at the burn unit," Matt said.

Pain flitted across the boy's face. "Months. But the folks was nice to me. They treated me good," he added quickly.

"And when you came home? Did people here treat you well?"

Jimmy grinned, what would have been a beautiful sight if the right side of his face had responded as the left had. "The ladies brought me so many cakes and pies, we had to give some to the neighbors."

"And the kids at school?" Matt asked gently.

The grin faded, replaced by such sadness Matt ached for the boy. "Some of 'em laughed at me. Called me names. All except Lizzie."

Lizzie McClain, Matt thought with a clutch in his heart. That little sweetheart knew the agony of being taunted about her looks. She wasn't about to inflict that misery on another.

"So . . ." Jimmy finished the last of his milk, hunched his shoulders, and wiped his mouth on his sleeve. "You gonna fix my face?"

The hope shining in the boy's eyes stabbed through Matt like a serrated blade. "That depends on a couple of things," he said and watched the hope die in Jimmy's eyes and his shoulders slump.

"Things like what?" Jimmy asked warily.

"I'll need your parents' permission to treat you, for starters."

"That's no problem. They want my face fixed. Ma, especially, so she won't cry no more when she looks at me."

Matt sighed. Apparently the boy hadn't heard the Dr. Wonderful gossip. And he wasn't about to explain that complex dilemma to an eight-year-old. "There may be a problem." Matt chose his words carefully. "Your parents may not want me to treat you. They were expecting Dr. Peyseur."

Jimmy nodded. "We met him last year. How come he didn't come back?"

"He broke his wrist and couldn't operate, so he sent me instead."

Jimmy thought for a minute. "Ma and Pa liked Dr. Peyseur. If he says you're okay, then that'll be good enough for them."

Remembering Becca's reports of the community's reservations about him, Matt doubted that. "Did Dr. Peyseur explain that fixing your face might take a long time? More than one operation over several years?"

"Yep, he sure did. That's why I'm anxious

to get started." The boy's clear gaze met Matt's without flinching. "The sooner the better. Will you do it?"

"I'll talk to your parents. We'll leave the rest up to them."

Jimmy nodded, apparently satisfied that all would be well. Matt didn't have the heart to discourage him. Besides, he intended to use all his persuasive powers to convince Mr. And Mrs. Dickens to let him begin. His fingers itched to start reconstructing the right side of Jimmy's face so it would be as appealing as the left. The boy was a good kid. He didn't deserve the stigma of his scars.

"Now —" Matt picked up the empty plate and glass "— you'd better buy your gum and go back to the church before your mother starts to worry about you."

Jimmy stood and flashed his endearing lopsided grin. "Thanks, Dr. —"

"Tyler."

"Thanks, Dr. Tyler. I'll see you soon."

Jimmy jumped from the dock and headed across the street to the store, his happy whistle floating back to Matt on the morning stillness.

"You okay, Mama?" Emily's voice seemed to come at Becca from a distance. "Mama?"

Becca blinked, seeing for the first time the book she'd been staring at for the past hour without reading a word. As she sat on the front porch in the pool of morning sunlight, her thoughts had centered on Matt and the unforgettable kiss he'd given her last night.

"Can I?" Emily asked, making Becca realize she'd been so preoccupied, she had missed entirely what Emily had said.

"Can you what?"

"Have lunch with Lizzie. Her mama said it was okay."

Becca started to protest that Emily spent too much time at the McClain house, then relented. Emily was Lizzie's best playmate, after all. The only one who didn't tease Lizzie about her cleft palate and strange speech. Becca had tried to instill in her daughter an acceptance of people as they were, and she was grateful that Emily gave Lizzie her unconditional friendship.

Besides, in the distracted mental state Becca was in, she might poison Emily unintentionally if she tried to feed her. "As long as it's all right with Mrs. McClain. But remember your manners."

Emily threw her arms around Becca's neck, planted a sloppy kiss on her cheek and skipped off the porch toward the McClains'.

Suddenly Granny's voice sounded in Becca's head, as clearly as if she sat in the rocker next to hers.

What have you gone and done, child? You itching to have your heart broke all over again?

It was just a simple kiss, Becca thought. No big deal.

Then why have you been in a trance all morning, like you've taken leave of your senses? Except your sense of smell, that is. I saw you bury your face in that sweater of his.

It had been years since a man had paid attention to her, Becca argued. Why shouldn't she be allowed to enjoy the sensation?

Might come to enjoy it too much. So much you won't want to let it go. What happens when Dr. Wonderful goes home to Hollywood?

When he left, she'd forget about him. After all, she had Emily and her job. She didn't need a man in her life to make it complete.

Took you a powerful long time to forget Grady, and him no good and not worth shooting. How long you think it'll take to forget a man like Matt Tyler?

All she'd have to do, Becca figured, was remind herself of the multitude of starlets Matt had returned to. That should clear her head fast.

And what about your heart?

Her heart wasn't an issue. She wasn't emotionally involved. Last night she'd simply enjoyed the company of an extremely handsome man.

Who smothered you with kindness. Was Grady ever that considerate?

Grady had his own agenda, Becca remembered, although she'd taken a long time to recognize that fact. Grady had cared only about Grady.

What's on the doctor's agenda?

Matt's intentions didn't matter, Becca insisted. He was nothing more than a summer fling. If that. He'd probably kissed her only because he felt sorry for her after she'd poured out her pathetic story.

But what a kiss.

Her bones melted at the memory of it, and she longed for another one.

She had to put a stop to her foolish thoughts.

She sprang from her chair and set her unread book aside. She'd trim the spirea hedge around the porch. The physical activity should drive her unwanted yearnings away and clear her head of Granny's warnings.

She was passing through the house on her

way to the barn for the loppers when the phone rang. The sound startled her, because folks in Warwick Mountain seldom used the telephone except in dire emergencies.

She grabbed the receiver with foreboding and a breathless "Hello."

"Hope I'm not interrupting," a deep, familiar voice announced.

"Matt?"

"Just had my phone installed. Had to try it out."

Angry at herself for the way her heart responded merely at the sound of his voice, she said dryly, "Seems to be working fine."

He must have registered the edge in her tone. "Don't hang up. There's something I want to tell you."

Her heart pounded against her breast-bone. Was he going to admit that she'd affected him as much as he had her? "I'm listening."

"I met Jimmy Dickens."

Swallowing the disappointment of her dashed expectations, she could almost hear Granny saying an I-told-you-so. "And?"

"He's a super little kid. We have to talk his parents into starting his facial repairs immediately."

She couldn't be angry with a man who appreciated one of her favorite students. "I agree. But it's going to be a hard sell. Mrs. Dickens is a pillar of the Baptist church. Your alleged reputation will be a real sticking point with her."

"I have to try. The boy deserves better than what life's dished out to him. I want to help."

The sincerity in Matt's voice was undeniable, and Becca felt her bones melting again. And her heart. How could she not be attracted to a man who cared about children and their suffering? "We could work in a visit to the Dickenses after seeing Lydia and the McClains tomorrow."

"I'll pick you up at one o'clock. That'll give us the entire afternoon. Got a pencil?"

"Why?"

"I'll give you my number."

"Tomorrow is fine. I won't need to call you back."

"I'm not thinking about tomorrow."

"Right," she said. "I'll have it in case someone needs a doctor."

"You'll have it in case you need me." An unidentifiable emotion weighted his voice.

"Emily and I are perfectly healthy —"

"I'm still concerned about those lights in the woods," he said. "I want you to call me if you see them again."

A warm, fuzzy feeling suffused her. "I

wouldn't want to wake you in the middle of the night."

"And I don't want anything happening to you. Call me, no matter how late. Promise?"

She couldn't resist his plea. "Promise." She jotted down the number.

"See you at one tomorrow." The line clicked as he hung up.

Becca replaced the receiver and leaned her forehead against the paneled wood of the hallway. "Oh, Granny, I think I'm in big trouble."

What kind of trouble, child?

Becca was beginning to realize just how wonderful Dr. Wonderful really was.

Matt hung up the phone. Just the sound of Becca's voice had made him ache to hold her again. Never had a woman fit in his arms as if he and she had been made for each other. Never had a mere kiss left him sleepless. Mere? Hardly. That kiss had been the stuff of legends. The contact had generated fireworks and rung bells. More than anything, he wanted to jump in his car this minute, drive straight to the Warwick farm and kiss her again.

He had promises to keep, however, so he forced himself to fasten his tool belt and return to the front room to install the last sheet of drywall.

As he crossed the threshold, the sight of a stranger perched on one of his sawhorses stopped him in his tracks.

"Dr. Tyler?" The man stood to face him.

The stranger had to be one of the locals, Matt realized. At least mid-seventies with weather-beaten skin, thick white hair and a tall lanky frame, he was dressed in denim overalls, a faded shirt and scuffed work boots. His hazel eyes seemed to spark with wisdom.

And guilt.

The stranger glanced toward the door as if afraid someone might spot him from outside.

"I'm Dr. Tyler. What can I do for you?"

"My name's Jake Bennett," the man said with a scowl. "I'm here about my sister, Lydia."

CHAPTER TEN

Matt suppressed his irritation, realizing the cat was apparently out of the bag about his sneak visit tomorrow. He wondered how Jake Bennett had found out.

Before Matt could say a word, however, Jake spoke again. "I could really use your help."

The man had him thoroughly confused. Was Bennett here about his sister or himself? "You need a doctor?"

"Right," Jack answered. "For my sister."

Matt quickly surmised that Jake didn't know about his wife's plans for Lydia after all, so he pretended ignorance as well. "What's her problem?"

"Sciatica."

"I can come now if you like." Matt reached to unfasten his tool belt.

Jake looked panicked and held up his hands. "Not so fast."

"Or we could pick a time that's more

convenient," Matt suggested easily.

"It'll have to be when my wife's not home."

"She doesn't want your sister to have medical attention?" Matt asked, continuing to pretend unawareness of the dynamics in the Bennett household.

Jake said, "I'm not sure she'd want you in the house."

"She have something against doctors?" Matt found himself appreciating the irony of the situation. Both husband and wife wanted the same thing, without each other knowing.

"She doesn't hold with men carousing with wild women," Jake said. "Not that I do, either," he added hurriedly, "but Lydia's problem is an emergency."

"What's carousing with wild women got to do with me?" Matt asked in fake innocence while tamping down his annoyance at the legend with which the magazine writer had saddled him.

"Delilah read about you in some news article," Jake said.

"You can't believe everything you read," Matt said mildly.

"Then it isn't true?"

"What isn't true?"

"That you dated all them movie actresses

181

out there in Hollywood."

"I definitely," Matt said with a straight face, "did not date *all* of them."

Jake Bennett was obviously no dummy and recognized when his leg was being pulled. His narrowed eyes accosted Matt with an accusing glance. "How many?" he demanded.

"None of your business."

"It is if my sister's going to be your patient."

"*Patient* is the operative word," Matt said hotly. "I want to cure her, not date her."

Jake gazed at him with a glimmer of respect. "You stand your ground, don't you, young feller?"

"I'm not a lecher, Mr. Bennett, and if your sister's in pain, I'd like to help."

"Lydia's not the only one in pain," Jake admitted. He sank onto the sawhorse, shoulders slumped. "She's a terrible patient and driving Delilah stark staring mad. But she's my own flesh and blood, so I can't turn her out of my house. Not while she's ill."

"I see your dilemma."

Jack scratched his head. "Problem is, how do we get you in without Delilah knowing about it?"

Matt took a moment to pretend to ponder

182

the situation. "I may have a solution. Your niece Rebecca has invited me to visit Delilah with her tomorrow."

"She has?" Jake looked surprised. "And Delilah agreed?"

"Becca assures me that your wife is one of the most gracious and hospitable women in Warwick Mountain."

"That's my Delilah, all right," Jake said with a glow of pride. "She'll accept you if you're Becca's guest." Then his expression sobered. "Do you think you can cure Lydia's sciatica? Nothing the Blairsville doctor prescribed has worked, and if I don't send her home soon, Delilah won't be speaking to me."

"While I'm at your house tomorrow, I'll talk to your sister and examine her and see what I can do," Matt promised.

"But not a word to Delilah or anyone else that I've talked to you," Jake demanded. "She'd nail my hide to the barn door."

"This will be our secret."

"Thank you." Jake rose, straightened his shoulders and extended his hand. Matt grasped it firmly.

As the old man was leaving, Jake turned in the doorway. "But no shenanigans," he warned, "or it'll be *your* hide nailed to the barn door."

Unable to decide whether he was more irritated or amused, Matt merely nodded, and Jake slipped away.

Matt looked at the drywall that needed hanging, but went instead to the phone in the back room to place a call to Steve Williams, his friend and colleague who specialized in back problems. Matt was caught dead in the middle of a family intrigue, but he also had his first patient in Warwick Mountain. Perhaps if he could alleviate Jake's sister's back pain, the Dickens and McClain families would be open to his treating their children.

He dialed Steve's number, hoping the neurologist would give him the knowledge he needed to ease Lydia's sciatica. Matt had to admit that curing her might also raise his stock a notch or two with Becca. If he intended to win the schoolmarm's approval, he would need all the help he could muster.

Late the following afternoon, Becca gazed with mixed emotions at the pile of shipping crates and packing boxes the UPS driver had just deposited on her porch.

"Dwight had promised us some supplies," she said to Matt, who climbed the steps behind her as they returned from their afternoon of visiting, "but I had no idea he'd be so generous."

"Not that you're likely to need them before next summer when Dwight returns." Matt sank into a rocker, clearly disappointed by the lack of progress the afternoon had yielded.

Becca feared he was right, but she tried to put a positive spin on the day's events. "At least you were able to help Lydia."

"We won't know that for a while," Matt said with a weariness she hadn't noted in him before. "After talking with the specialist and then examining Lydia, I'm almost certain she has a bacterial infection of the sciatic nerve. Even if my diagnosis is correct, the antibiotic I gave her won't take effect for a few days."

Determined to raise his spirits, Becca perched on the porch rail in front of him. "But once it does, when folks see how you've helped her, maybe they'll give you a chance."

With a dubious expression, Matt tugged his fingers through his hair. "Maybe. But I doubt a sciatica cure will be enough to persuade Lizzie's or Jimmy's parents. You were there. You saw how adamant they were."

Matt's disappointment was palpable, and Becca fought the urge to wrap her arms around him and comfort him. Their visits with the two families had been polite but strained, and neither couple had budged an inch on allowing Matt to treat their children.

"Their conditions aren't life-threatening," Matt said, "so their parents are willing to wait until next summer for Dwight. They don't want a reprobate touching their precious little ones." Anger filled his voice and caused the chiseled planes of his face to darken. "What kind of monster do they think I am?"

"They don't think you're a monster," Becca said quickly. "But you have to remember where you are. Folks around here take womanizing seriously."

"Womanizing?" Matt snapped with annoyance. "Is that what I am, a womanizer? Just for dating beautiful women?"

Becca shrugged, fighting the jealousy that bubbled inside her and regretful that she'd stirred his anger, but she'd opened this can of worms and had to deal with it. "That magazine article implied a great deal more than dating."

"Okay," Matt admitted, his temper flaring. "But I've always been clear about my intentions, and that there were no strings attached."

Becca sighed. "That's the problem. You're

in a different world here, caught in a clash of cultures."

He shook his head. "These people are human, too, with the same wants we all share."

Becca felt her own face redden. "I'm walking proof of that."

"I'm sorry," Matt said instantly, "I didn't mean to imply —"

"I concede your point," Becca said quickly with more calm that she felt. "And it's true these people aren't saints. Everyone falls short of the mark now and then. The difference," she added gently, "is that when we ordinary folks do, it isn't overblown and published in a national magazine."

"What about forgiveness?" Matt demanded with obvious frustration. "Isn't that important, too?"

"You just said how human these folks are. Forgiving doesn't come easy for most of us." Becca thought for a moment. "Folks, too, are afraid."

"Of me?"

If the topic hadn't been so serious, Becca would have laughed at the astonishment on his face. "No, not of you. They're afraid of being ostracized. Accused of guilt by association."

"But if I can help their children —"

"They don't see it that way. As you said,

Lizzie and Jimmy aren't in danger, although both children are suffering emotionally from their disfigurements. They bear the taunts and teasing of the other children, the knowledge that they're different. Maybe their parents don't want to add to their embarrassment by having them treated by a man with a questionable reputation."

"I'm a doctor," Matt said, his anger at defeat evident, "not a sociologist. I don't have the skills to deal with a culture clash. I might as well take the next plane back to L.A."

Becca's heart stuttered at the possibility. "Your being here still helps."

"I don't know how."

She poked the nearest packing crate with her toe. "Look at all the work you've done at the feed store. If you set up this equipment and inventory these supplies, Dwight will be able to go straight to work when he arrives next summer."

She tried not to think of her neighbors who might be spared complications of serious illnesses if they'd allow Matt to examine and treat them now. Or of Lizzie and Jimmy enduring another year of cruel taunts.

"You could have hired a carpenter for building the office," Matt said glumly. "Doesn't take a medical degree to frame a few walls."

"But I *couldn't* hire a carpenter," Becca said with sincerity and more warmth than she'd intended. She glanced at her hands, clasped in her lap, to hide her feelings from him. "Couldn't afford one. I want you to know how much I appreciate all you've done."

She lifted her head again, and his eyes met hers. An unmistakable current flowed between them. His glum expression disappeared, replaced by a soft smile that made her weak.

"If you're trying to make me feel better," he said lightly, "it's working."

"Stay for supper?" Becca was reluctant for him to leave, yet she was afraid of her own reactions if he remained. She made the offer, almost hoping he'd turn her down. "It's the least I can do to make up for your dismal afternoon."

"You keep feeding me wonderful meals," he said jokingly, "and I'll grow so accustomed to great cooking, you'll have to marry me."

"You keep asking," Becca replied in the same bantering tone, "and I'll *have* to say yes."

A look of surprise seemed to jolt through him, and she wondered if she'd crossed the line in her teasing.

"I'd better get supper started," she said quickly and hopped from the porch rail. "You might want to load these boxes in your car while it's still light."

Without a backward glance, she escaped to the kitchen before she said or did anything else foolish.

Talk about a clash of cultures.

How could she allow herself to be so deeply affected by a man whose world was so different from her own? She had no future with Matt Tyler. And unless she wanted to end up with her heart broken, she'd better etch that fact in her mind and use it as a shield against Matt's appeal.

Three days later, Becca parked in front of the feed store and steeled herself for seeing Matt again for the first time since the evening of their unsuccessful visits. She'd enjoyed too much having him at her table that night. Had appreciated too much his easy interaction with Emily, his sense of humor, his insistence on clearing the table and washing the dishes. To her dismay, Becca had found herself fantasizing about Matt as a permanent fixture in their lives — until the cold, hard reality of their situations had kicked in again.

Different worlds, different values.

No future in that.

"What did you say, Mama?" Emily asked beside her.

Great, Becca thought, the man had her crazy, talking out loud to herself. "Nothing, sweetie. Let's go see what Dr. Tyler's been doing to the feed store."

"What about the picnic?" Emily asked.

"This won't take long."

Becca left the car, unbuckled Emily from her seat in the back and held the girl's hand as they climbed the stairs. The double doors stood open to the morning breeze, but no sounds emanated from the building.

When they stepped across the threshold, Becca gasped in surprise.

"Wow!" Emily said. "Dr. Matt did all this?"

"He's a miracle worker." Becca took in the waiting area Matt had set up in the front half of the store. An attractive, brightly colored area rug delineated the space on which chairs, sofas, tables and lamps had been arranged. One corner held a low table covered with books and toys and surrounded by chairs designed for children.

Beside the door to the doctor's office sat a desk, topped with a telephone, an appoint-

ment book and a sign that read Receptionist.

"What do you think?" Matt's deep voice
asked beside her.

"Hi, Dr. Matt," Emily said.

"Hey, short stuff," Matt answered.

Becca had been so enthralled by the
store's transformation, she hadn't heard him
enter the waiting room. "I can't believe how
much you've accomplished. This is wonderful."

Matt's shrug emphasized his broad shoulders, but disappointment, not nonchalance,
glimmered in his eyes. "Amazing what you
can do when nothing else claims your time."

"Emily." Becca pointed to the table in the
corner. "Why don't you see what books Dr.
Tyler bought."

"Okay." The little girl skipped across the
room, settled in one of the petite chairs and
selected the largest picture book from the
pile.

Becca turned back to Matt, giving herself
a strong silent reprimand not to be taken in
by his warm brown eyes and heart-stopping
good looks.

"I'm sorry I haven't had better luck at
recruiting patients," she said. "I've called on
several families to encourage them to see
you, but no luck. I'm hoping when more of

them meet you at the picnic today, they'll change their minds."

"Swayed by Dr. Wonderful's irresistible charm?" Matt asked with a grimace.

"Stranger things have happened." Becca knew she was counting on nothing short of a miracle.

The folks of Warwick Mountain were good people, but stubborn and clannish. So far, no one had proved willing to break from the herd and step forward to accept Matt's medical treatment. In a sense, they were cutting off their noses to spite their own faces — since most would profit from a medical exam — but they saw themselves instead as banding together to keep out a bad influence.

Becca hoped that meeting Matt and seeing him as a real person instead of some Hollywood fantasy might change some minds. He would only be in Warwick Mountain three more weeks before returning to his practice, and she was running out of time.

She thrust away the thought of how empty her life would seem with Matt on the other side of the country instead of just down the road.

"I've talked with Dwight," Matt said, "and explained the stone wall I've run into."

"Did he have any advice?"

"Just to keep on as I have been. He agreed, like you said, that at least the clinic will be up and running when he arrives next summer."

"So he's planning to come back?" Relief flooded Becca. She'd feared the community's rejection of his partner might change Dwight's attitude.

"He loves this place," Matt said, as if there were no accounting for taste. "He's talking about retiring here."

"I don't suppose you'd consider coming back?" The question popped out before she realized what she was saying, and Becca could only hope Matt hadn't picked up on the longing in her voice.

He shook his head. "What would be the point?" He grinned at her, an expression so delightful, her heart flip-flopped at the sight. "You don't need a carpenter anymore."

"Thought you might want a few more home-cooked meals," she teased.

"For those, I would take the red-eye in a heartbeat." He leaned toward her, and for a moment, she thought — hoped — he was going to kiss her again. He'd kissed her when he left after supper the other evening, but it had been a friendly kiss, a brief brush of his lips across her own when he'd said goodbye and thanked her for the meal. That brief contact had left her dreaming of a life she couldn't have, craving the very thing she knew she should avoid.

Culture clash, remember? Granny's voice rang in her head. *With heartache to follow.*

Becca stepped away from Matt and temptation, glad they'd soon be surrounded by a crowd. The presence of others would prevent her from doing something foolish. "I hope you're hungry now. The ladies always compete at the Fourth of July picnic, trying to outdo one another with their cooking."

"Can we go now, Mama?" Emily had crossed the room and was tugging on her hand. "I want to see Lizzie. She's waiting for me."

"Okay, sweetie. Ready, Matt?"

Matt nodded. "You're sure I don't need to bring something?"

"I have enough food in the car for a family of eight," Becca said.

Matt flexed his arms in a circus strongman parody. "Then you'll need somebody to . . . tote, is that the word? . . . all those goodies for you."

Becca couldn't resist laughing, couldn't suppress the happiness that bubbled inside her, couldn't help looking forward to spending the rest of the day in his company. He might be leaving her life forever in a few weeks, but if she guarded her heart, she could enjoy his company now. And later she'd have the memories.

"The car's parked out front," she said. "We can walk to the church from here."

With Emily bouncing in excitement at her side, Becca opened the car for Matt to remove the picnic basket and cooler, then fell in step beside him.

"Look, Mama," Emily observed in her high, piping voice that carried on the breeze. "We're just like a real family."

"You and I *are* a real family," Becca assured her. "We always have been."

"But now we have Dr. Matt for a daddy," Emily said.

"No, Emily." Becca could feel the unwanted flush spreading across her cheeks. "Dr. Matt's our guest today."

"Oh, Mama." Emily's face crumpled in disappointment.

Matt leaned down and whispered in the little girl's ear. Emily giggled with delight, slipped her hand from Becca's and ran ahead of them toward the church, where a crowd was already gathering on the grounds.

"What did you say to her?"

Matt flicked Becca a casual glance. "I told

her she could pretend I'm her daddy, just for today."

"Oh, Matt, you shouldn't have."

"What's the harm?"

"Knowing my talkative child, she'll tell everyone at the picnic that you're her father."

"But they'll know that isn't true."

"No, they won't."

He stopped short, his eyes wide with amazement. "You don't really think people will believe I'm Emily's biological dad?"

Becca closed her eyes and groaned. "After that magazine article, they probably already believe you've sired half the children in the state of California. And that's just for starters."

Matt set down the cooler and basket and called to Emily. When she returned to them, he knelt to meet her, and she threw her arms around his neck. "Can I call you daddy?"

"No, sweetheart," Matt said with a gentleness that touched Becca's heart. "I can be your pretend daddy today, but it has to be our special secret. Nobody else can know."

Emily's mouth puckered in a frown. "Not even Lizzie?"

Matt shook his head. "Not even Lizzie."

Tears appeared in Emily's eyes. "You

won't do the three-legged race?"

Matt raised his gaze to Becca in question.

"It's a father-daughter event," she explained.

"I can do that," Matt said to Emily. "We'll race together. And I bet we can win."

Emily's tears disappeared. She hugged Matt, broke away and scanned his face. "You won't forget?"

"Cross my heart."

Her happiness restored, Emily skipped ahead of them again.

"Thank you," Becca said.

"She's a great kid. Too bad she doesn't live in California."

"So you could see her more often?"

"So she wouldn't feel like she needs a daddy," Matt observed. He nodded toward the crowd on the grounds. "Here, traditional family values are alive and well. Everywhere I look I see a mother, father, and two-point-five children. In southern California, nuclear families are anything from two guys or two gals to a single mother with kids, or a young professional couple with dogs."

"I like a traditional family," Becca admitted, "and I missed being part of one when I was growing up."

"Then maybe you should find Emily a daddy," Matt said in the same casual tone he'd used earlier.

"What should I do?" Becca replied, keeping her voice light to hide her annoyance. "Advertise in the personal section of the Asheville paper? After all, I don't meet any eligible men in my line of work."

"Aren't there male teachers at your school?"

Becca laughed. "I'm the only teacher at my school."

Matt gazed at her in disbelief.

"It's true," Becca insisted. "I teach in a one-room schoolhouse that's over a hundred and fifty years old. I have sixteen students, grades kindergarten through five. When the students reach sixth grade, they're bussed to the school in town."

Matt shook his head. "You are living in a time warp."

"I love it," Becca insisted. "And the best part is that I can take Emily to work with me. She's part of the preschool class."

"No single men living on Warwick Mountain?" To Becca's discomfort, Matt had returned to his earlier topic.

"Young people here either marry and settle down right out of high school or head for the towns and cities. Life's hard on the mountain. Many can't wait to escape."

"Why not you?"

"Marry and settle down?"

"Escape," Matt clarified.

"Been there, done that. Made me realize that this is the life I want for Emily and me." She relaxed, grateful Matt had finally abandoned trying to locate a husband for her.

"What about widowers?" he asked, returning to his original topic like a dog to a bone.

"What about them?"

"Any here that might make good husbands?"

Becca arched an eyebrow. "How come you're so interested in marrying me off?"

"If I can't practice medicine," he said with a killer smile, "I have to do something useful."

"Widowers," Becca said thoughtfully, playing along. "As a matter of fact, Mr. Jamison is the most eligible widower on the mountain. Owns more land than the rest of us combined. Been looking for a good wife for years."

To Becca's delight, a scowl flashed over Matt's face before he managed to hide it. "Fond of this Mr. Jamison, are you?"

"Yes, I am." That was no lie. She'd adored the man all her life.

"Thought about marrying him?" Matt's question was so offhand, it was funny.

Becca held back a smile. "I'm not qualified."

"I don't believe that," Matt said with
enough feeling to make her tingle. "You
have everything a man would want in a
wife."

Her spirits soared at his praise, but she
shook her head. "Not Mr. Jamison."

"Then he's an idiot," Matt said hotly.

"No, he's not," Becca said with a laugh.
"He's ninety-nine years old and just moved
into an Asheville assisted-living facility. The
man needs a nurse not a wife. I'm definitely
not qualified."

Matt's expression was rueful. "You've
made your point."

"Which is?"

"That'll teach me to stick my nose in
other people's business."

"Just help Emily win the three-legged race
and you're forgiven," Becca said.

They'd reached the church grounds.
Crepe-paper banners of red, white and blue
were strung between the trees and around
the bandstand. On tables under the long
covered shelters built for outdoor dinners,
women were unloading baskets and coolers.
Children and even a few dogs chased each
other through the throng of people. On the
other side of the church at the athletics

field, a group of young boys had lined up. At the bandstand, Art Ledbetter announced the beginning of the foot race, his loud voice tinny and crackling over the ancient sound system.

"Rebecca!"

Becca turned at her aunt's voice calling her name, and Matt halted beside her. Delilah rushed toward them from the food tables, her sister-in-law, Lydia, in tow, moving with amazing speed and agility for a woman they'd last seen bedridden.

"It's a miracle!" Delilah declared when she reached them. "A godsend! Dr. Tyler, you've put Lydia back on her feet."

Jake's gray-haired sister beamed at them. "I'd be dancing today —" Her expression soured. "Except Jake's so strict, he doesn't hold to it."

"The antibiotics worked." Matt's pleasure at Lydia's recovery was obvious.

"They sure did," Lydia said. "Now that I can take care of myself, I'm itching to go home. I have a hundred and one things demanding my attention."

"You'll never know how much I appreciate what you've done," Delilah said, then quickly added, "I couldn't bear to witness Lydia in such pain any longer."

"Just doing my job," Matt said. "Wish others would take advantage of that while I'm here."

"They will," Lydia said. "I intend to tell everyone I see today how you've helped me."

The women walked to the tables with them, and Matt deposited Becca's cooler and basket onto the nearest empty space. She was in the midst of unloading them when she realized he was no longer at her side. She shrugged, figuring he'd slipped away to begin meeting folks, when Art Ledbetter's voice blasted from the public-address system again.

"Listen up, folks," her neighbor announced. "I got Dr. Tyler up here with me, and he wants to say a few words."

Becca felt her knees give way, and she sank onto the nearest bench.

She had no idea what Matt was about to say, but whatever it was, she wished he'd cleared it with her first. She watched as Matt stepped to the edge of the bandstand, took the mike and cleared his throat.

CHAPTER ELEVEN

Matt stared at the sea of upturned faces that surrounded the bandstand and wondered whether his spur-of-the-moment inspiration was a good idea. But with everyone's attention riveted on him, there was no backing out now.

He glanced toward the picnic area where Becca watched him, her worry visible even from a distance. He recognized other people in the group — the McClains, the Dickenses, Bobbie Jo from the Shop-N-Go, and Jake Bennett, standing with a bunch of his friends who'd been admiring someone's coon-hound puppies in a kennel in the back of a battered pickup truck.

Three teenage girls edged closer to the bandstand and studied him, exchanging giggling comments behind their hands.

Now or never, Matt thought, took a deep breath and spoke.

"Hello, everyone. I'm Dr. Matthew Tyler,

and if I haven't met you already, I hope to meet you today. But first I want to bring you greetings from Dr. Peyseur and to offer his apologies for not being here this summer as he'd promised. He can't perform surgery now with his broken wrist, but he's asked me to assure you that his wrist will mend and he'll be here next year."

A murmur of sympathy went through the crowd, testimony to Dwight's high standing in this tightly knit community. Matt wondered briefly how the old man had managed to bridge the barriers, then returned to his speech.

"For those of you who don't know, I'm Dr. Peyseur's partner, and he's asked me to fill in for him this summer."

Another murmur rippled through the crowd, and Matt could only imagine what people might be saying.

"At the request of Ms. Warwick, your schoolteacher," he said, "I've refurbished the old feed store, which will serve as a clinic. I've had a phone installed —" Matt recited the number slowly, then repeated it. "So if you need medical care, you can either drop in at the clinic or call for an appointment."

He noticed that no one had bothered to write down the phone number.

"I look forward to talking with each of you today." With a sinking feeling in the pit of his stomach, Matt handed the microphone back to Art Ledbetter. He'd only wasted his time and possibly made a fool of himself by his public plea. The crowd stood stone-faced.

Until a faint sound from the picnic tables carried across the grounds.

Applause!

Matt glanced to where Becca sat. She wasn't clapping, merely looking as stunned as he felt. His gaze swept to the left of her where Delilah and Lydia were beating their hands together like wild women.

A noise to the front of the bandstand joined with their applause. Directly before him, Emily, Jimmy and Lizzie were clapping like crazy and cheering at the top of their lungs.

"Welcome, Dr. Tyler!" Jake Bennett hollered from over by the pickup truck.

A smattering of polite applause then traveled through the crowd. Feeling slightly less humiliated, Matt jumped from the bandstand and headed toward Becca.

With a few notable exceptions, his reception had been chilly, but it was a start.

Becca walked to meet him. "I almost had a heart attack, wondering what you were going to say when I saw you take the mike."

"Fools rush in," he admitted. "I decided I didn't have anything to lose and might even gain a few patients by making a public intro. I wasn't exactly a rousing success."

"Displayed your courage," Becca noted.

"Or my arrogance, depending on how it's interpreted."

"We'll find out," Becca said. "Come on. I'll show you around and introduce you."

A blur of names and faces filled the next hour as Becca helped him work the crowd. The adults were courteous and respectful, and the children, especially the younger ones who were obviously smitten by their teacher, were friendly, but Matt couldn't help noticing the reserve among the grown-ups.

"Thanks for filling in for Doc Peyseur," Lloyd Pennington, an elderly farmer said, not unkindly, but he asked for neither advice nor an appointment for treatment of his visibly painful rheumatoid arthritis.

As the old man hobbled away, Matt turned to Becca. "Anywhere we can escape to?"

"Escape?"

"If I have to shake another hand or smile at another person who obviously disapproves of me, I won't be responsible for my reactions," Matt said through gritted teeth.

Becca's expression was sympathetic. "I know just the place. Follow me."

She called to Emily to stay with Aunt Delilah, then she and Matt threaded their way through the crowd, crossed a wide expanse of green, skirted the edge of a cemetery, filled with ancient headstones, that rose on a hill beside the church, crossed a playing field of hard-packed dirt and entered a grove of mature hickory trees. When they exited the other side of the grove, they crossed a field to reach what appeared to be an old rock quarry. Matt stepped to the edge, looked down and saw deep blue water sparkling twenty feet below.

"This must make a great swimming hole," he observed.

Becca tramped down a portion of the high grass on the quarry's edge and sat down. Matt sank beside her, legs stretched before him, his face turned upward to the sun and breeze. The spot was a paradise. An open field of wildflowers bordered the quarry, gentle folds of mountains rose behind it, and the air that filled his lungs was invigoratingly fresh and crisp. High clouds did little to mask the brilliant blue of the sky. Even though it was the middle of summer, the breeze held a refreshing coolness.

"No swimming," Becca said. "Kids are

forbidden to come back here."

"Why?"

"Because none of them knows how to swim."

For Matt, who'd swum every day in the Pacific for the past ten years, the inability to swim was inconceivable. "Why don't they learn?"

"Primarily they don't have time. Farmers' children work the land most of the summer. Also, there's little need for them to know how to swim. Most of the water around here is in creeks, not deep enough for swimming."

"What about this place?"

"Too dangerous. Too deep. And with the steep quarry walls, there's no easy access, even if the kids could swim. Every parent makes it off limits."

Matt glanced around, noting signs of recent visitors in the trampled grass. "Somebody comes here."

Becca smiled. "The older teenagers sometimes come here after dark. Without their parents' knowledge or permission, of course."

Matt studied the woman beside him, lying back on her elbows, her face turned to the sun, eyes closed, honey-colored hair stirred by the breeze. "Did you ever come here?"

He was suddenly and unaccountably jealous of any teenage boy in her past.

Becca opened her eyes wide. "Are you kidding? Granny would have skinned me alive."

"So you've never been kissed here before?"

Her lips parted slightly, her cheeks reddened, but her gaze held his. "Never."

"Then it's about time."

He lowered his head and kissed her. Cupping her face in his hands, he reveled in the smoothness of her skin, her warmth, and the immense satisfaction of connecting with a beautiful woman he admired and respected.

Respected too much to risk her reputation by kissing her in broad daylight where anyone might see.

Reluctantly, he drew back. Her green eyes gazed at him, puzzled.

"You mustn't think that I wanted to stop," he said.

"Then why did you?" she asked, her voice barely more than a whisper.

He wanted to keep kissing her until the stars fell out of the sky.

"I remembered that tricky little clause in your teaching contract. The one on moral turpitude." He smiled and caressed her cheek until she smiled in return. "If I were a kid, and my favorite teacher showed up with a strange man at a picnic, you know what I'd do?"

She shook her head, a quzzical expression on her face.

"I'd follow them," Matt said, "to find out what they were doing."

"Oh, no!" Becca sat bolt upright, ran her fingers through her hair, then gazed over her shoulder toward the woods with a worried scowl. "Did you see anyone?"

"No."

"That doesn't mean no one was there. These little devils are skilled hunters, woodsmen. They could be watching us now and we wouldn't know."

"Next time I kiss you," he said, "I'll choose a more private place."

"There won't be a next time." Her words were sharp, final.

"There's always a next time," he insisted.

"Not for us."

"Why not? We're both adults."

"But why kid ourselves? There's no future for us. You're going back to California. I'm staying here."

"Why does there have to be a future?" he asked. "Didn't you enjoy kissing me?"

"Yes, but —"

"Then we'll kiss again, just for the fun of it."

She shook her head, her frustration clear. "Don't you understand? If there's no future in it, if it doesn't lead to more, it ceases to be fun."

"What do you mean by more? Love?"

"No!" She pressed her lips together tightly. "Well, yes, but —"

"But you look at love as a lifetime commitment," he said softly, remembering all she'd told him about mountain values.

"It should be. That's what I was taught."

Matt plucked a blade of sweet grass to chew, leaned back on his elbows and gazed across the deep blue of the water that filled the quarry. He didn't understand Becca's point of view, but he respected it. Respected her. More than any woman he'd ever met.

With a twinge of discomfort, he realized his unnamed dissatisfaction had returned. It had disappeared during the time he was building the clinic. Either that or he'd been too busy to notice it was still there, but now his discontent had reappeared with a vengeance.

It couldn't be romantic frustration. He'd suffered the same uncomfortable feelings in California when he'd had his pick of beautiful partners. He'd hoped a break from the rigors of his practice, even if he'd missed his South Pacific cruise, would ease his discomfort, but nothing so far had worked.

So what was bugging him?

"I'm sorry if my beliefs offend you," Becca said.

"What?" Matt shook off his gloomy introspection.

"We were talking about relationships and you turned inward. Are you okay?"

"No," he admitted to his surprise. "I'm not."

"You're not sick?" Becca placed her wrist against his forehead, and he reveled in the cool sensation of her skin against his.

"Not physically. But I'm beginning to wonder whether I need a good shrink."

Becca's eyes twinkled with mischief. "I thought everyone in la-la land had his own therapist."

"They do," he agreed in an attempt to lighten the conversation, "but it's rough fitting the therapy time in between visits to the plastic surgeon and workouts with a personal trainer."

"Seriously —" Her expression sobered. "If you want someone to talk to —"

"It won't violate your moral turpitude clause?"

She grinned. "I guess that depends on what you want to talk about."

Matt tossed the blade of grass aside.

"That's the problem. I don't know what's bothering me. For the past year or so, I've suffered this vague discontent that I can't put my finger on."

"Discontent in your work or your personal life?"

He couldn't believe he was spilling his guts to Becca. He'd never talked to anyone like this before, not even Dwight, who was like a father to him. "I wish I knew. If I could narrow down what's eating at me, maybe I could identify it and make it stop."

"Sounds like you don't take enough time to think," Becca said.

Matt blinked in surprise. "You're right. This past week is the most laid-back schedule I've had in years."

"Haven't you had vacations?" The genuine concern in her voice, the interest sparking in her eyes warmed him, made him want to keep talking. Sharing.

"I always needed a vacation from my vacation after I returned home," he said.

"Maybe that's the bright side of having no patients the next three weeks," she suggested. "You'll have plenty of time to think."

He resisted the impulse to pull her into his arms. "You're good at this."

"What?"

"Therapy. Listening. Maybe you should

hang out a shingle."

Becca laughed, a lovely silvery sound that echoed off the quarry walls. "Folks here are shy enough of medical doctors. How many clients do you think I'd have as a therapist?"

"You could pencil me in for several hours a day for the next three weeks."

He meant every word. Not that he wanted her to psychoanalyze him. He'd discovered that he simply enjoyed her company, even if they were doing no more than sitting in the grass in the sunshine. He didn't need Hollywood premieres or five-star restaurants or an exotic island paradise to hold his interest. Becca Warwick managed to keep him entranced all on her own.

"Mama!" Emily's voice sounded from the edge of the hickory grove.

Becca turned toward her daughter. "You're not supposed to come here."

"I'm staying away from the quarry. But I need Dr. Matt! It's time for the three-legged race."

"Promises to keep," Matt said. He stood, tugged Becca to her feet and kept her hand in his until they reached Emily, Lizzie and Jimmy Dickens who waited for them in the shade of the trees.

Becca experienced mixed feelings returning

to the crowded picnic grounds. Glad on the one hand to be freed from temptation, she had to admit she had valued her time alone with Matt.

Had particularly enjoyed his kiss.

Too much.

No one, not even Grady, had affected her the way Matt did. If he hadn't been the one to pull away, she probably would have kissed him for the rest of the day. No telling what public scandal might have resulted if they'd been spotted.

Ahead of her, Emily skipped alongside Matt, chattering happily. He'd been wonderful with her daughter, and the guilt over Emily's fatherless state that sometimes rose up and confronted Becca gnawed at her now. Matt would make a good dad, she found herself thinking.

Then wondered if she'd lost her senses.

What woman in her right mind would want Dr. Wonderful as the male role model for her child?

She reminded herself that all she'd seen of Matt Tyler had been outside of his usual environment. No, he hadn't hit on any of the women in Warwick Mountain — if she didn't count his kissing her — even though his natural charm and incredible good looks had turned several heads. But the straight-

and-narrow life he'd led since his arrival could be attributed more to lack of opportunity than a reversal of character.

As hard as she tried, however, she couldn't picture the Matt she knew living the free-wheeling, irresponsible life the magazine article had painted of a man flitting from woman to woman like a worker bee through a flower garden. Had he been grossly misrepresented by his interviewer, or had the soft spot for him in Becca's heart generated a corresponding soft spot in her brain?

She gave herself a mental shake. The true state of Matt's character was immaterial. Even if he lived as celibate as a monk, the gulf between them was inseparable. He was a man apparently addicted to fun and fame with the money to gratify his every whim. Becca, on the other hand, believed in hard work, frugality, and helping her neighbors. They had nothing in common.

No matter. In three weeks, he would be gone.

And, she realized with an uncomfortable jolt, she was going to miss him more than she wanted to admit.

All the more reason to keep her distance and forget the summer fling she'd briefly contemplated. But the sight of him on the playing field with her daughter made her resolutions hard to keep.

Matt knelt beside Emily, tying the little girl's leg to his with cotton strips for the three-legged race. Whatever he was saying was making her giggle, and her face shone as if she'd already won first place.

Whatever his other faults, Becca thought with a sigh, he was wonderful with children. Too bad he hadn't chosen pediatrics as his specialty.

The participants for the age ten-and-under father-daughter three-legged race assembled at the starting line, and a crowd of mothers, relatives and other supporters gathered at the sidelines. Matt held Emily firmly by the hand. When the official gave the starting signal, Matt released her, and, as if they'd prearranged the maneuver, she wrapped her arms around his leg that was tied to hers.

Five-year-old Lucy Ledbetter and her father, Art, immediately took the lead among the six pairs of contestants.

Becca noted that Lizzie McClain stood on the sidelines, not competing in her age bracket. Her lack of participation was no surprise. The child rarely engaged in any activity that drew attention to herself. Becca felt a surge of resentment toward the McClains and their prejudice against Matt that prevented Lizzie from receiving the surgery she needed. Becca yearned for the day that Lizzie could interact with the other children without feelings of inferiority or embarrassment.

Her resentment was soon overtaken by excitement when Matt and Emily left the other teams behind and gained on Art and Lucy Ledbetter. Emily's face was red with the attempt to run as fast as she could, and Matt's face showed his strain, probably reflecting his efforts to temper his superior strength and speed to match Emily's.

The noise of the crowd thundered around Becca as the people cheered on their favorites. Susie Ledbetter's screech of excitement almost burst Becca's eardrum.

"Go, Emily," Becca yelled. "Run, Matt!"

Emily glanced toward her and stumbled, but Matt kept her from falling.

They gained on the Ledbetters, and for a moment Becca thought they would pull ahead to win, but both pairs crossed the finish line at the same time.

"A tie!" the official announced.

Matt tugged loose the strips that bound Emily to him, scooped her in his arms and twirled her around. Becca rushed to join them.

"We won!" Emily screamed with delight.

"Mama, we won."

"We won, too," Lucy said, beaming with pleasure.

"Congratulations." Matt extended his hand to Art Ledbetter. "A good race."

Art shook Matt's hand with polite reserve. "Thought for a minute there you were going to beat us."

Matt shook his head and grinned. "You had too good a lead for that."

The official awarded both pairs a blue ribbon, and Matt pinned theirs to the front of Emily's T-shirt.

"I never won anything before," Emily said. "Thanks, Matt."

"Don't thank me," Matt said. "I couldn't have entered the race without you. You were a great partner."

"Can I show Aunt Delilah?" Emily asked.

Becca nodded. "And wait at the tables for me. It's time to eat."

Emily ran on ahead, and Becca stayed behind with Matt as the crowd dispersed from the field and wandered toward the picnic tables.

"You made her day," Becca said. "Thank you."

"I can't remember the last time I had so much fun," Matt said with obvious sincerity. He looked like a kid himself with his face flushed with victory, his hair tousled, his eyes shining. "Emily's a great little trooper. I had no idea she could move so fast."

"You two were great together. Toward the end, I thought you were going to beat Art and Lucy."

A guilty look scudded across Matt's face.

Becca cocked her head and considered him. "You could have won, couldn't you?"

"Was it that evident?"

She shook her head. "Only because I was watching you and Emily so closely. Did you hold back?"

He nodded.

"Why?" she insisted.

"I knew the locals wouldn't think kindly of a stranger horning in on their glory. There's enough animosity toward me already."

Becca felt her temper flare. "But what about Emily? She had her heart set on winning that race."

"And she did, didn't she?" He grinned, and her anger fizzled. "Believe me, I wouldn't have let her down. When I realized we could tie with the Ledbetters, I decided a draw was the best solution for everybody."

Becca sighed and shook her head again. "I don't know whether I should hug you or hit you."

Matt's grin broadened. "One would definitely be worth the other."

Becca had to admit, if only to herself, that she was tempted. "How about I feed you instead?"

"I could eat a horse." His smile transformed into an apprehensive look. "That's not a Southern delicacy, by any chance?"

Becca bristled at the comment, then caught the mischief dancing in his eyes. She laughed and swatted him playfully on the arm. "Behave yourself."

His reciprocating grin warmed her to her toes. "Did you bring fried chicken?"

"Can't have a picnic without it."

"I plan to eat myself into a coma."

"What a thing for a doctor to say."

"What a way to go is how I look at it."

As they approached the picnic tables, Lyla Dickens met them. "Have you seen Jimmy?"

"Not since before the race," Becca said.

Susie Ledbetter joined them. "I can't find Lucy. She was here a minute ago."

The entire group turned at the sound of a scream emanating from the hickory grove. Jimmy Dickens burst through the trees, running as fast as his short legs would carry him and shouting at the top of his lungs.

"Lucy fell in the quarry. She's drowning!"

CHAPTER TWELVE

"We went to find my pocketknife I dropped," Jimmy howled. "I told Lucy not to go near the edge, but she didn't listen."

Matt caught Susie Ledbetter as her knees sagged beneath her and thrust the woman toward Becca and Lyla.

"Call the paramedics," he said, "and have someone bring rope to the quarry. Lots of it."

Without a backward glance, he set off at a run, his legs eating up the distance, his mind working furiously, trying to gauge how long he would take to reach the girl, trying not to think of the short time without oxygen before her brain would be damaged. Or how her lungs would fill with water —

He pushed himself harder, oblivious to the clamor of voices and activity behind him. Slowing only when he reached the quarry's edge, he jerked off his shoes while he scanned the surface for Lucy. Sunlight glinted off golden curls briefly before they disappeared beneath the cold, dark water.

Matt pushed off from the edge in a dive that brought him as close to where the child had been as possible without landing on her. The frigid water shocked his system and took his breath away, but all he could think of was the frightened little girl who couldn't swim, who, even if she could reach the water's edge, would never be able to climb the perpendicular twenty-foot walls to escape the quarry.

He treaded water and with a twist of his neck, slung his wet hair away from his face.

"Lucy!" he screamed.

The child was nowhere in sight.

Desperate to find her, Matt dived beneath the surface only to realize he could see nothing in the water's dark depths.

Becca handed Susie Ledbetter to Lyla Dickens, yelled to Aunt Delilah to watch Emily and took off after Matt. From the corner of her eye, she could see Uncle Jake and several other men running toward their trucks. She hoped someone would have the rope Matt had demanded.

On the other side of the grounds, the preacher sprinted for the church and the telephone in the office to call the rescue squad.

Matt had run so fast, Becca lost sight of him until she broke through the trees. She caught only a short glimpse of him on the edge of the high cliff before he catapulted over the quarry's edge.

Her heart in her throat, she raced to the rim. Neither Matt nor Lucy was anywhere in sight, and only a slight ripple on the serene water indicated either had been there.

Becca considered jumping in to help, but her own swimming lessons had been limited to navigating the length of the pool in her college physical-education class. In spite of her good intentions, with her inexperience, she might end up simply another victim needing rescue.

"Where is she?" Art Ledbetter spoke behind her. "I can't see her."

The agony in his voice cut through Becca like a sword, making her thank her stars that Emily wasn't lost in the lake. She closed her eyes and hoped against hope that Lucy and Matt would survive.

She turned from her anxious scan of the water to identify the bustle of activity behind her. Uncle Jake and several of his friends had arrived, carrying several lengths of rope. With skillful hands, they knotted the various strands together into one long piece with a loop at the end.

Becca turned back to the water, searching frantically for life. The wait seemed endless, the silence deafening, and knowing that everyone watching felt as desperate and helpless as she did. Afraid to witness his pain, she couldn't force herself to look at Art Ledbetter, but she couldn't ignore the tortured gasp of his breathing, the only sound on the still air.

Suddenly, like an orca whale ascending from the depths at a Sea World attraction, Matt broke the surface, gasping for air. When the crowd spotted the golden-haired bundle in his arms, a cheer rang out, reverberating against the surrounding peaks.

"Toss that rope down there," Uncle Jake ordered.

Someone heaved the rope over the edge, and Matt, with Lucy in tow, swam toward it. He slipped the noose over his head and under his arms.

"Not you, Tyler!" Art yelled. "Send up the girl first!"

Matt, treading water while supporting Lucy, shouted back, "She'll be battered against the rock wall if she comes up alone. Pull me out with her, and I can protect her."

Uncle Jake apparently saw immediately the sense of Matt's plan and organized a team of men to haul on the rope. Matt swam to the foot of the rock cliff, positioned Lucy in his arms, and, as the men above him pulled, braced his feet against the rock for the treacherous twenty-foot climb.

Becca watched, unaware she was holding her breath. Matt grasped the girl firmly, holding her away from the jagged wall. She could see the muscles of his legs working as he painstakingly walked his way up the wall, held almost perpendicular to the rock face by the tension of the rope from above.

When he neared the rim, Uncle Jake, Art and several others hauled him over the side. Tears streaming down his face, Art grabbed Lucy from Matt's arms.

"Oh, God!" The father's cry of agony stopped everyone short. "She's dead!"

"Is Lucy in heaven with Granny?" Emily asked that night when her mother tucked her into bed.

Becca swallowed hard against the grief welling up in her throat. How could she explain the death of a child to another child when she couldn't wrap her mind around the concept herself?

"We'll talk about it in the morning," Becca

promised, hoping by then to find some way to clarify the inexplicable.

Art Ledbetter's anguished cry still rang in her head, tore at her heart. Matt, exhausted as he'd been, had sprung immediately into action and begun CPR with reassuring calmness and authority. He'd worked without ceasing, continuing even once the rescue squad arrived. She hadn't had a chance to speak with him because he'd continued his ministrations all the way to the ambulance. Once they'd reached it, he'd climbed inside with Lucy without missing a beat in his resuscitation efforts for the ride to the hospital in town.

The picnic had ended. No one had the heart left for food or fun, and everyone had scattered, returning home to wait for the final news on little Lucy Ledbetter. Becca still hadn't heard. She'd called the hospital twice, but both times the woman at the nurses' station had been professionally noncommittal, which Becca had taken as a bad sign.

Knowing she couldn't sleep, Becca wandered into the kitchen to fill the kettle and put it on to boil. She'd brew a cup of Granny's special herbal tea, the one that calmed nerves and induced sleep, and hope it would make her rest.

She kept seeing Matt in her mind's eye, tenderly cradling Lucy's body to protect her from the jagged rocks, absorbing the buffeting and resulting cuts and scrapes with his own body as the men pulled the dripping pair from the quarry. He had worked like a madman to restore the child's breathing, refusing to break his concentration even when Becca had placed a blanket around his wet, shivering shoulders.

Becca's dream had been to bring a doctor to Warwick Mountain, a healer who would keep her friends and neighbors safe, so people wouldn't die before their time as Granny had. Now, she realized with a sob, that a doctor couldn't always save his patients, even when he wanted to so desperately, as Matt obviously had while he wrestled with death to breathe life into Lucy.

A knock at the front door broke through her thoughts and filled her with icy dread. Even though Becca was expecting the worst, until she actually heard the final news, she could always hope that Lucy had somehow, miraculously, survived.

With leaden feet, she trudged to the entryway and flipped on the porch light. The dim glow illuminated Matt, wearing rumpled green hospital scrubs in place of his formerly sodden clothes, his face grim, weariness apparent in his stance. She opened the door.

"Sorry to bother you so late." Fatigue weighted his voice. "But I couldn't face returning to the feed store alone just yet."

Becca stood aside to let him in. "Come back to the kitchen. I was just fixing a cup of tea."

She closed the door behind him, turned off the porch light and forced herself to ask, "Lucy?"

The weariness in his face transformed into a smile unlike any she'd ever witnessed, and his shoulders straightened as if he'd thrown off his exhaustion. "We think she's going to make it."

Unable to believe what she'd heard, Becca sank onto the deacon's bench before her legs gave way. "But I thought . . . Art said she was dead."

"She'd stopped breathing, but not long enough to cause brain damage." He rubbed the back of his neck and rolled his shoulders, reminding Becca of the strain his muscles must have taken from his climb out of the quarry. "If she makes it through the next twenty-four hours — and her prognosis is good — she should be fine."

Joy and relief flooded her. Lucy had been like her own child, a neighbor since birth, a student in her preschool, her daughter's friend, her friends' daughter. She leaped to her feet, wrapped her arms around Matt and hugged him with all her might.

"Dr. Tyler, you *are* wonderful!"

Matt pulled her close, gripped her tightly, and then pulled back far enough to see her face. "It wasn't me. The entire staff of doctors was waiting at the hospital when we arrived."

Becca shook her head. "You're too modest. You pulled her from the quarry. You performed CPR. Without you, the other doctors would have been useless."

"I was the logical choice," Matt said. "After what you'd told me earlier, I realized I was probably the only one at the picnic who could swim."

"You deserve a medal," Becca said, dizzy with relief and happiness, drunk with gratitude and admiration. "A statue in the town square."

A disarming grin crooked the corner of his mouth. "Warwick Mountain doesn't have a town square."

"Then we'll have to think of something else." With her arms still around him, her face inches from him, Becca pretended to concentrate, but his closeness proved too distracting.

"I've thought of something else already," he said.

She didn't have to ask.

Granny's voice rang in her head. *Haven't you had enough heartache in one short life without setting yourself up for more?*

He saved Lucy's life, Becca argued silently.

And he'll ruin yours.

Not if I don't let him.

Matt kissed her, drowning out Granny's warnings, obliterating Becca's ability to think.

With a jolt, she realized she was feeling more than just attraction.

She loved this man.

Loved his intelligence, his sense of humor, his willingness to risk his life for a little girl he barely knew, his generosity in abandoning his exotic vacation to fill in for a friend and help a community of strangers, his clear affection for her daughter.

Loved the way he made her feel when his arms wrapped around her. Loved the way his smile made happiness zing through her as if she'd drunk too much blackberry wine.

A shrill, insistent warning shrieked suddenly in her ears, and she jerked away from him.

But the alarm continued.

Disoriented, she gazed at him in confusion.

"Your kettle's boiling." His voice was as breathless as she felt.

He had her mind so scrambled, she hadn't recognized the sound. "I'd better stop it before it wakes Emily."

But she couldn't tear herself away from the disquieting comfort of his arms.

He released her and gave her a gentle nudge down the hall. Like a sleepwalker, she wandered into the kitchen, removed the kettle from the burner and turned off the stove.

The shrill whistling ceased, and the quiet was overwhelming. Becca stood in front of the refrigerator and placed her burning forehead against the smooth, cool surface of the door.

Had she lost her mind?

As much as she loved and admired Matt Tyler, the prospect of a life with him held no more permanence than the presence of the summer lightning bugs that flitted outside the kitchen window. In the greater scheme of things, he was merely a blip on her radar screen, a temporary distraction, a man who would walk out of her life as quickly as he had entered, with no looking back, no possibility of ever becoming anything more than a haunting memory.

And what was she to him?

Just another in a long line of women who had passed in and out of Dr. Wonderful's existence like travelers catching a connecting flight at an airport. Matt Tyler was a way station, not a destination.

Steeling herself, she turned, only to bump against Matt, who had come in behind her.

"You okay, Becca?"

His arms went around her again, and try as she might, she didn't have the strength or will to push away. She shook her head against his chest and forced herself to speak. "I can't do this."

He placed his hands on her shoulders, held her at arm's length, and lifted her chin until their gazes met. "I love you, Becca."

Without success, she attempted to stifle the joy his words brought her. Forcing herself to recall every salient detail of the magazine article she'd read about him, she twisted her mouth into an ironic grimace and accused him with narrowed eyes. "How many women have you said that to?"

"None." The piercing gaze of his remarkable brown eyes didn't waver. "You're the only one."

"Do you really expect me to believe that?" Much as she wanted to, she didn't dare.

She couldn't risk the hurt if he was lying.

"It's the truth." He hesitated then, as if remembering.

Her heart sank. There *had* been others. She was nothing special. Just another in an endless stream of conquests.

"If you don't count my mother," he added. "Although, I never told her often enough."

"Oh, Matt, I want to believe you —"

"But you are definitely the only woman I've ever asked to marry me."

His proposal took her breath away, and for a moment, she thought for sure she'd heard wrong. "What did you say?"

He pulled her closer, nestling her chin in the hollow of his neck, resting his cheek on her hair. "I want you to marry me, Becca."

She'd heard right, but she couldn't believe it. "You're kidding."

"I've never been more serious about anything in my life."

She reveled in his embrace, savored the security of his arms, treasured the beat of his heart against her face, but his proposal left her too stunned to think. "I don't know what to say."

She lifted her head from his chest and stared into the face of the man she'd come to love, wondering if she could take a chance, a risk. What if she did? What if she *didn't?*

Then she'd have the memories, Becca thought, memories of the only man she'd ever really loved. Grady had been a horrible mistake, an overgrown boy who'd used her and deserted her. Matt was a mature man . . . one who was ready to settle down.

With her.

With Emily.

In spite of his apprehensive expression, Becca couldn't mistake the love shining in his eyes, the sincerity ringing in his voice.

He loved her.

"Will you marry me?" he asked again.

CHAPTER THIRTEEN

Matt waited for Becca's answer. He wouldn't pressure her. They'd known each other only a short while, and if she needed time to make up her mind, he'd give her all the time she wanted.

After all, it was only a few hours ago that he'd realized himself that he wanted to spend the rest of his life with Becca. Waiting in the hospital for word on whether Lucy Ledbetter would live or die had completely and unexpectedly changed his perspective, had made him recognize what was truly important.

He'd had enough of mindless social events, vacuous women and single living. He wanted someone to share his life, and he knew without a doubt that someone was Becca Warwick. He didn't mind that she came with a ready-made family. In fact, Emily was an asset, because Matt had come to love the little girl as well as her mother. He couldn't wait to show them both California, to teach Emily how to swim, to walk on the beach at sunset with Becca, and to sleep every night and wake every morning with his wife snuggled in his arms, while the Pacific surf crashed against the shore outside their bedroom window.

He might even cut back on his hours at the office and hospital to have more family time.

Family.

The word offered comfort, happiness and promise.

Beside him, Becca sighed.

"You don't have to give me an answer now," he assured her. "Take time to think about it."

"I can't leave Warwick Mountain," Becca said with an intractable set to her jaw.

"Sure you can. You'll love California."

Becca pulled away and gazed at him with worried eyes.

"I could never live in California," she said bluntly.

He didn't like the turn the conversation had taken. "It's not a foreign country."

"California may be a nice place to visit," Becca said gently, "but I don't want to live there."

"How do you know?" He tried without

success to keep the irritation from his voice. "You've never been."

"California's not the problem."

His spirits plunged. "If you don't love me —"

Her fingers against his lips stopped him from saying more. "I love you, Matt. But I have responsibilities I can't fulfill in California."

"If it's Emily you're worried about, I want to adopt her. Give her my name, too. We'll all be Tylers. And she'll have the daddy she wants."

Becca shook her head sadly. "I don't know if I can make you understand. Emily isn't the problem, although I admit I'd rather she grew up in Warwick Mountain than Beverly Hills."

His blood turned cold. "What is the problem?"

"It's me. I can't leave here."

"Why not?"

"My roots are here. Warwicks have been on this mountain for almost three hundred years, long before the American Revolution. The place is in our blood."

"You can keep this place. We can visit here on vacation." He was determined to shoot down every objection, hurtle every obstacle.

"But I have a promise to keep, one I can't

honor in California."

"Your clinic?"

She nodded. "I swore on Granny's grave that I would see the clinic built and make certain it always served the people of Warwick Mountain."

"You could make arrangements for the clinic long distance. Use phones, faxes, email." He couldn't understand her devotion to a place and its people. "If you need more time to set things up —"

"I need to be here," she said solemnly, her tone unyielding. She appeared to think for a moment and her expression brightened. "You could live here with Emily and me."

He shook his head. In all the plans he'd formulated yesterday, Becca and Emily had come home with him. He'd never contemplated moving. "Stay here? And do what? Not much call for cosmetic surgery here, even if folks were willing to let me treat them. Which they're not."

"But if they were —" Her gaze scoured his face. "Would you want to live here?"

Matt hesitated. As much as he loved Becca, could he renounce the familiar pleasures of California living? Was his discontent temporary or could he really do forever without the surf, sun and sea? Would he miss too much the cultural stimulation of art galleries, famous restaurants, film premieres and the rich and famous who frequented them?

Her eyes sad, Becca stroked his cheek. "Maybe we should forget you ever proposed. We're like oil and water, you and me. Not a good mix."

Her observation wounded him, primarily because of the truth of it. They might as well have been born on different planets. He pulled her close and pressed his lips against her hair, not wanting to ever let her go. "Then what are we going to do?"

She released a deep sigh. "Accept the fact that we were never meant to be."

He trailed his fingers over the exquisite smoothness of her skin, then tangled them in her hair, gazing into magnificent eyes that swam with tears.

"I won't accept that."

"Then what will we do?" she asked.

"We'll kiss," he answered gently. "At least one more time."

Leaving Becca was the hardest thing Matt had ever had to do, especially when all he wanted was to wrap his arms around her and hold her close forever.

Assuming too much, not thinking things through, he'd bungled his proposal. Big time. Becca had been clear in her refusal, adamant about the impossibility of either of them belonging in the other's world. Although he believed she loved him, he also believed she had accepted they'd never be together.

Matt couldn't accept it. Wouldn't. He'd find a way to bring them together somehow.

He stared at the darkness through the uncovered kitchen window, trying to think. A distinct flash of light in the distant woods caught his eye.

The midnight intruder had returned.

If he couldn't convince Becca to marry him tonight, at least he could protect her. He turned to find her watching him in the darkness.

"Call 911," he said.

Her eyes clouded in confusion. "Are you ill?"

"Someone's in the woods. I'm going after him. Call the sheriff."

He started to rise, and she grabbed his arm. "You've been hero enough for one day, Matt. Let it go."

Bending low so their lips almost touched, Matt spoke with fierce conviction. "I have to satisfy myself that whoever's out there isn't a threat to you and Emily. If they are, I'll need the sheriff's help."

He kissed her, hard and fast, then sprinted out of the house.

Stunned, Becca sat for a second, then moved into action, racing to the phone in the hallway.

She gave her name and location to the dispatcher and explained about the prowler.

"We have a deputy in the area," the dispatcher said. "He should be there within fifteen minutes."

Becca hung up and started to go after Matt. Then she remembered Emily asleep upstairs. With the prowler a potential threat, she couldn't leave Emily alone in the house. Instead of following Matt, she locked the kitchen door, then hurriedly secured the other doors and windows on the first floor.

That action took only minutes. Becca stared through the kitchen window toward the woods, where the bobbing light still shone, wondering what was happening, fearful for Matt's safety.

The intruder was probably harmless, she assured herself, but common sense demanded otherwise. If the person had legitimate business in her woods, why wait until midnight and sneak through the darkness?

Who would do such a thing? Her imagination fired into overdrive — a moonshiner brewing illegal white lightning; a poacher hunting animals on the endangered-species list; a serial killer hiding bodies —

Stop it! she ordered herself before she descended completely into hysteria.

But she couldn't help worrying about Matt, couldn't help longing to hold him safely in her arms. She couldn't marry him — they were oil and water as she'd told him — but she could wish with all her might that he'd be protected from harm.

As she watched, the light in the woods suddenly went out. Turning on her heel, Becca raced to the mantel in the living room, took down Grandpa's shotgun, then scurried to the closet in the guest bedroom where she kept the shells in a combination-lock box. In her desperation, she at first forgot the series of numbers, then, once she remembered them, fumbled with clumsy fingers. At the sound of pounding on the back door, she dropped the box on her bare foot.

"Becca, it's me!" Matt called. "Open up."

She picked up the gun and box and hurried to the kitchen. Flipping on the porch light, she gasped at the sight of a strange face peering through the window with a grimace. Then she spotted Matt behind the stranger, wresting the man's arm behind him in a grip he couldn't escape.

Becca opened the door, and Matt shoved the stranger into the kitchen. Squinting in the sudden bright light, the scrawny stranger appeared to be between fifty and sixty years old with his long gray hair pulled back into a ponytail. In bell-bottom jeans and a tie-dyed shirt, he looked like a throwback to the sixties. His already anxious expression intensified when he glimpsed Becca's shotgun.

"Please," he begged. "Don't shoot me. I wasn't hurting anyone."

"Sit down and don't move." Matt released the man, who sank immediately into the chair Matt had indicated and began rubbing the arm Matt had wrenched.

"What were you doing in my woods?" Becca asked.

"Stealing," Matt said before the man could answer. He held up a bulging gunny-sack and tossed it to Becca.

Afraid of what she'd find, Becca peeked inside. The contents amazed her. She turned to the man. "Roots? You were digging up and stealing roots?"

With a crestfallen expression, he nodded.

"Why?" Becca insisted. "Were you hungry?" The man's gaunt frame suggested hunger might be a possibility.

To her surprise, the man laughed. "Don't

you know what those are?"

Matt stood protectively between Becca and the stranger, obviously poised to put a hammerlock on the thief if he made a threatening move.

"They're roots," Becca said.

"Very valuable roots," the man replied. "What's in that sack is worth several hundred dollars."

Becca snorted in disbelief. "What fool would pay that for roots?"

The man's shoulders drooped. "No one, now that you've got them."

"You'd better explain yourself, mister," Matt said in a voice that made even Becca cringe.

"Yes, the sheriff's on his way," Becca added. "He'll be here any minute."

"You're pressing charges?" the stranger asked.

"Depends," Matt said, "on what you were doing on Ms. Warwick's property."

"Look," the man said with a forced smile. "I'm not a criminal. I'm a businessman."

"What kind of business has you trespassing in the wilderness in the middle of the night?" Matt demanded.

"Herbs."

"Herbs?" Matt and Becca asked in unison.

"I own a shop in Asheville. We sell organic

produce, herbs and New Age books." He nodded toward the sack. "Those are ginseng roots. Highly valued. Very expensive. The woods back there are full of them."

"Ever occur to you to ask permission to dig there?" Matt said with a heavy dose of sarcasm. "Or to offer to pay for the ginseng you took?"

The man had the decency to look ashamed. "I thought it was public land."

"And that would make it all right?" Matt asked with obvious disgust.

"The national forest is farther west," Becca said. "The land where you were digging is mine."

"Look," the man said pleadingly. "Maybe we can work out a deal."

"A little late for that, don't you think?" Matt said.

He looked so fierce, so protective of her that Becca again experienced what it would be like to have someone watch over her.

It felt good.

Too good.

She couldn't afford to become accustomed to the feeling. When Matt returned to California, she and Emily would be looking out for themselves, totally on their own again.

A shadow on the back porch caught

Becca's eye, and a uniformed deputy stepped through the open door into the kitchen.

"You got a problem, Becca?" The deputy was Billy Thornburg. He'd been three years ahead of Becca in school, and she'd known him all her life.

"This is Dr. Tyler." Becca introduced Matt. "He —"

"You're the one!" Billy's face lit up like a Christmas tree. "Man, the whole department's talking about you. That was some amazing rescue, pulling Lucy Ledbetter out of the quarry."

"The greater achievement was pulling me out," Matt said. "If it hadn't been for Jake Bennett and the others, Lucy and I would both be feeding the fishes."

Billy eyed the stranger, cowering in the chair. "What's the problem, Doc?"

Between them, Becca and Matt explained about the ginseng thief. Billy cuffed the stranger and prepared to lead him away. "We'll run a background check. See if he's got a record."

"If he hasn't," Becca said, taking pity on the man's obvious terror at being arrested, "I don't want to press charges. Not if he'll promise to stay off my land."

Billy nodded. "It's your call."

Becca thanked the deputy and locked the door behind him.

She turned to Matt. "Thank you, too."

He shook his head. "I didn't do it for you. I did it for me. I couldn't stand worrying about who might be out there, who might be threatening you and Emily."

"Then thank you for caring about us."

She didn't have the will to resist when he pulled her into his arms and kissed her.

Nor did she have the will not to cry when he left.

Becca awakened early, disoriented at first after the events of the night before. Then she remembered her conversation with Matt, and was filled with incredible longing.

And regret.

Sudden anger suffused her. Had she lost her mind falling for another man she'd never marry? When she'd succumbed to Grady's charms, she'd been young, foolish and inexperienced.

So what's your excuse now? Granny's voice rang in her head. *Foolish is the only one that still fits.*

Becca threw back the covers and pulled on her clothes from the night before. With any luck, she would have herself showered and dressed before Emily awoke.

What had happened between her and Matt already seemed unreal. The incredible joy and satisfaction of expressing their love for each other, and the total unexpectedness of his proposal, had caught her completely by surprise.

If they both hadn't been so deeply affected by Lucy's accident, none of the above would have happened, she assured herself. They had allowed their heightened emotions to cloud their judgment, carry them away.

It had taken the trespasser's appearance in the woods to ground them both in reality again.

By the time she'd had her shower and dressed, Becca had convinced herself that Matt's proposal had been a total aberration, an experience that should be treated as if it had never happened.

But how could she purge last night from her mind when her heart cried out in anguish at the impossibility of saying yes?

You've faced tougher challenges before, Granny's voice assured her. *You're a Warwick. You can do anything you set your mind to.*

It wasn't her mind that worried her, Becca grumbled. It was her heart. She'd lost it irretrievably to the handsome doctor.

Then marry him and go to California.

Even if she could bear to leave Warwick Mountain, Becca thought, how could she be sure that Matt had been serious, that proposals of marriage weren't just part of the line that Dr. Wonderful spun for all his conquests?

Do you really believe he wasn't sincere?

No, Becca thought, but did she trust in his sincerity because he'd spoken the truth or because she wanted so desperately to believe he'd meant the words? She didn't want to think she'd allowed herself to be duped.

Again.

And agonizing over it wouldn't accomplish anything except driving her crazy. Granny had always said the best solution for dealing with whatever worried you was keeping busy, so Becca decided to bake a coffee cake for Emily's breakfast. While it baked, she called the hospital to check on Lucy's overnight progress.

By the time Emily appeared in the kitchen for breakfast, the hot-from-the-oven coffee cake with drizzled icing, along with a vase of fresh flowers just picked from the garden, adorned the table.

"Is it somebody's birthday?" Emily asked.

Becca shook her head. "I just thought

251

you'd like something different this morning."

"Where's Dr. Matt?"

"What?" Becca viewed her daughter with alarm. She had checked on Emily after Matt left, and she'd appeared to have slept through the stranger's capture and Billy Thornburg's carting him away.

"I thought I heard Dr. Matt last night," Emily said.

Becca decided not to tell Emily about the ginseng thief. She didn't want her frightened. "Matt dropped by to tell us that Lucy's going to be all right."

Emily's whoop of delight rang through the kitchen. "She didn't die?"

"I called the hospital this morning, and she's doing fine. She'll be coming home in a few days."

Emily slid into her chair and accepted the filled plate her mother handed her. "Dr. Matt saved her. I knew he would."

"Yes, he did."

"Dr. Matt can do anything."

He'd done some pretty amazing things last night. Becca pushed the memory of Matt's proposal from her mind. "Eat your breakfast. Aunt Delilah and Uncle Jake will be here to pick you up soon."

"Where are we going?"

"To Blairsville to take Lydia home now that she's better."

Yesterday, convinced that Lucy Ledbetter had died, Becca had asked Delilah to take Emily with them, knowing the community would be mourning and preparing for a funeral. She'd wanted to spare Emily from as much as possible.

Today, however, with Lucy recuperating, Becca wished she hadn't arranged for Emily's trip. Now she wouldn't have her daughter's company to distract her from thoughts of last night.

"Dr. Matt fixed Lydia, too, didn't he?" Emily asked.

"Yes, he cured her back problems."

Emily drank her milk, then wiped her face with her napkin. "He can do anything. I hope he fixes Jimmy and Lizzie."

Becca opened her mouth, planning to explain that Matt wasn't omnipotent, but the ringing of the phone interrupted her.

"Becca," Matt's voice said in a strangely muted tone when she answered, "you have to come down here right now."

She thought immediately of Lucy. "Is something wrong?"

"I'm swamped," he continued in the same whispering voice, "and I'm desperate for help."

"Swamped?"

"Patients. They're lined up at the door and the phone's been ringing off the hook since seven-thirty. I need someone to organize appointments and answer the calls."

"Mama," Emily called, "Aunt Delilah and Uncle Jake are here."

Becca spoke into the phone. "I'll be there as quickly as I can."

Minutes later, with Emily waving from the back seat of the car as Uncle Jake drove away, Becca headed for her own vehicle.

What a mess she'd landed herself in.

How could she possibly *not* think about last night if she was spending the day with Matt? She could only hope the press of patients, their prejudice against Matt apparently set aside by his rescue of Lucy, would provide a buffer to protect her from her rebellious heart.

July was drawing to an end, and with it, Matt's time on Warwick Mountain. He shoved the last article of clothing into his backpack and scanned the room that he'd called home the last several weeks. Not that he'd had much time to spend in it.

Ever since the Fourth of July picnic, he'd worked long hours, finally able to accomplish what he'd come here to do. Looking back, he still found the dramatic turnaround in attitude toward him hard to believe.

As satisfying as the work he'd completed, however, had been having Becca close by. Since the day patients began arriving, she'd filled in as his receptionist. They hadn't spent any real time together, but just seeing her smile when he entered the waiting room, and hearing her voice as she answered the phone, had seemed so right, as if she should always be within arm's reach.

But not any longer. Today was his last on Warwick Mountain.

"I can't thank you enough for what you've done for all of us." As if conjured up by his thoughts, Becca stood in the doorway.

"Sure you won't change your mind and come to Asheville with me?" he asked.

She shook her head. "You'll be busy with the surgeries, and I'd only be in the way at the hospital."

"Jimmy and Lizzie could use your support. They're both crazy about you." *And so am I.*

"Their parents will be with them. I'll visit when they come home after their operations."

Was her refusal an effort to spend less time with him, an effort to make a clean break?

He crossed the room toward her, but she held her ground, her arms folded across her chest. "Becca —"

"I know what you're going to ask, Matt. I can see it in your eyes."

"Then say yes this time. Marry me."

Sadness filled her eyes. "We promised not to go there. To pretend you never asked."

"I can't. And I don't believe you can either. Do you love me, Becca?"

"Don't do this, Matt."

"Just answer my question."

Her gaze met his, unflinching. "Yes."

"Then this isn't over. I'll be coming back for you."

Before she could protest, he drew her into his arms, kissed her with a fierceness that sent his senses reeling, then let her go.

Without another word or a backward glance, he left the building, climbed into the Land Rover and drove away.

CHAPTER FOURTEEN

Nine months later

Spring had come to Warwick Mountain.

Apple trees blossomed on the hillsides, bright yellow sprays of forsythia swayed in the breeze, and the creeks ran high with snowmelt from the mountaintops.

Becca stood in the doorway of the schoolhouse and watched her students disperse for the day. Emily walked between Lucy and Lizzie, the three girls chattering and giggling, their high, excited voices thrown back to her on the wind.

Matt had worked a miracle with Lizzie. At the Asheville hospital after he'd left Warwick Mountain, he'd repaired her cleft lip and palate so that even the most astute observer couldn't tell that the defect had ever existed. And he'd arranged and paid for a speech therapist to retrain Lizzie to form her consonant sounds, utilizing her newly formed hard palate. Her speech wasn't perfect yet, but good enough that she'd lost her shyness about talking to the other children. Now she was a normal, happy little girl.

And Jimmy Dickens, although he'd require more operations before his scars were less evident, had gained confidence from the improvement in his appearance — and the fact that he received weekly letters from Dr. Matt, the hero who'd saved Lucy Ledbetter's life.

Jimmy and Lizzie were the most obvious examples of Matt's successes, but the mountain was filled with others. When Matt had risked his life for Lucy, the community had embraced him as one of their own. Lloyd Pennington swore he felt twenty years younger since Matt had provided him with free medication for his rheumatoid arthritis, and the Habersham sisters took great pride in telling everyone that Dr. Tyler had pronounced them "fit as fiddles."

Becca leaned against the doorjamb. Matt had cured everyone but her. He'd left her with a hole in her heart she could never fill. Almost ten months ago, he'd promised he'd come back for her, but she hadn't heard a word.

Not a phone call. Not even a letter.

"You look so down in the mouth, honey.

Did somebody die?"

Delilah stood in front of her. Becca had been so lost in thought, she hadn't seen or heard her aunt trudge up the hill to the school.

Becca shook her head and forced a smile. "What brings you here?"

"Do I need a reason to visit my favorite niece?"

"Reason? No. More like an ulterior motive."

Delilah pretended to look insulted. "Guess you're not interested in the latest news, then?"

Becca really wasn't. In fact, she hadn't had much interest in anything since Matt had gone away. As much as she'd tried to convince herself he'd been no more than a summer romance, his leaving had taken the sunshine from her life. For Delilah's sake, however, Becca tried to look interested.

"What kind of news?"

"The Jamison farm is sold."

Becca nodded, unimpressed. Old Mr. Jamison had died in the nursing home last August. He had no surviving family, so the sale of his estate came as no surprise.

"Mountain Outreach Corporation bought it," Delilah said.

"Never heard of them."

"That's just the thing." Her aunt's eyes glimmered with curiosity. "Nobody else has either. And not only that, bulldozers have already started clearing the south pasture, getting ready for some kind of construction. Bigger than just a house."

"If it's an industry, it'll mean new jobs," Becca said. "New jobs will keep more of our young people from moving away."

"And bring traffic, pollution and who knows what else," Delilah said with a grumble. "We need a committee to look into this."

"Count me out," Becca said.

Delilah cocked her head and studied her. "You still pining away for that good-looking doctor?"

"I'm exhausted from dealing with a roomful of overactive children all day."

"You ever hear from him?"

"Susie Ledbetter will probably help with your committee," Becca said, ignoring her aunt's question. "After all, her land's closest to the old Jamison property."

"Let him go, child," Delilah said, refusing to let her off the hook. "He's back in California where he belongs. He did us all a heap of good while he was here, but I doubt we'll ever see him again."

"Thanks for bringing the news, Aunt 'lilah. I'll tell Susie you want to talk to her."

Delilah gave her a hug, pecked her on the cheek and stalked back down the hill, apparently ready to do battle with the mysterious Mountain Outreach Corporation. Becca, glad to escape her aunt's astute scrutiny, returned to her classroom.

After erasing the blackboards, straightening rows of desks and watering the pot of tulips blooming on the windowsill, she was stuffing the night's paperwork into her briefcase to carry home, when a noise sounded at the front door.

A tall man stood in the doorway, silhouetted by the late-afternoon sun, his face in shadows.

Becca felt a tremor of uneasiness. She was alone, miles from anyone, with a man she didn't know, one who definitely wasn't related to any of her students.

"May I help you?" she asked.

"You don't recognize me?"

She recognized his voice instantly — and the disappointment in it, even before he stepped into the light where she could view his face. He looked even more handsome than she'd remembered, but leaner, with a difference she couldn't put her finger on.

"Matt!"

For a moment, she feared she would faint

from surprise. Taking a deep breath, she eased herself into the chair behind her desk.

"What are you doing here?" She was pleased that her voice carried none of the turmoil tumbling inside her.

His brown eyes burrowed into hers, held her fast, and her breath caught in her throat. "I told you I'd come back for you."

Anger flashed through her at his words. Nothing had changed. She wasn't going to California. All his presence accomplished was to reopen a wound that had never really healed. "We've been through all that. We're at the same impasse. Always will be."

He walked toward her, rounded the desk and sat with his hip propped on the edge. "Always is a long time."

She refused to be dragged into this emotional quagmire. "Have you seen Lizzie? And Jimmy? They're doing wonderfully."

"I plan to visit both of them. And everyone else I treated last year."

"Early vacation?" she asked.

"Dwight and I have closed our practice."

His announcement hit her as if a wall had fallen in on her. "You've given up medicine?"

He leaned toward her, took her hands that were clasped in a white-knuckled grip atop her desk. "I've decided to practice real medicine, thanks to you."

"I don't understand." She was drowning, her head swimming, overcome at the proximity of him, the warmth of his hands, the love shining in his eyes.

"Years ago, I decided to study medicine because I watched my mother die a slow, agonizing death, unable to afford the proper care that might have saved her. Somewhere along the line, I lost sight of my purpose. I let money and fame and excitement derail me. But last summer, working with people who really needed my care, I rediscovered what I'd known at the beginning. I want to be a healer."

Becca frowned. "That's why you gave up your practice?"

"So Dwight and I can open a new one." He stood and pulled her to her feet. "We bought the Jamison property."

"*You're* Mountain Outreach Corporation?" She couldn't tell whether his startling news or his closeness was causing her dizziness, her sense of unreality.

"We're building a hospital. We plan to fly in children from all over the country — all over the world — who need reconstructive surgery. We'll provide the service at no cost. And our hospital will also contain the emergency clinic you've always wanted."

He was building her clinic.

Granny's clinic.

Her legs sagged, and she would have fallen if he hadn't caught her. "But that will cost a fortune."

"Dwight and I have file drawers full of names of grateful clients with more money than they know what to do with. We've formed a foundation. It's already funded. All we're waiting for is the completion of the building."

The meaning of his words suddenly hit her. "You'll be living here?"

"For the rest of my life."

"But you never called, never wrote. I thought you'd —"

"Forgotten you?" His palms caressed her cheeks. "Not a chance. I wanted to make certain everything was in place before I told you. Things just took longer than I'd hoped."

She still couldn't believe what was happening, that Matt was really here, really staying. "How could you leave California?"

"Oh, Becca, loving you, how could I not? Will you marry me now?"

"If you don't mind living in an old log mountain house."

"I'd live in a cave if I could be with you."

He kissed her then, lifting her off her feet.

You'll do, young man, Granny's voice sounded in Becca's mind. *You'll do just fine.*

Matt pulled back suddenly and stared at her wide-eyed. "Did you hear someone?"

"A ghost," Becca said with a grin, her heart overflowing with happiness. "A very friendly ghost. But don't pay any attention to her. Just kiss me again."

She didn't have to ask twice.

ABOUT THE AUTHOR

Charlotte Douglas

The major passions of Charlotte Douglas's life are her husband — her high school sweetheart to whom she's been married for more than four decades — and writing compelling stories. A national bestselling author, she enjoys filling her books with love of home and family, special places and happy endings.

With their two cairn terriers, she and her husband live most of the year on Florida's central west coast, but spend the warmer months at their North Carolina mountain-top retreat.

The employees of Thorndike Press hope you have enjoyed this Large Print book. All our Thorndike, Wheeler, and Kennebec Large Print titles are designed for easy reading, and all our books are made to last. Other Thorndike Press Large Print books are available at your library, through selected bookstores, or directly from us.

For information about titles, please call:
  (800) 223-1244

or visit our Web site at:
  http://gale.cengage.com/thorndike

To share your comments, please write:
  Publisher
  Thorndike Press
  10 Water St., Suite 310
  Waterville, ME 04901